# ALIEN ALLIANCE

CAROL MELBER

ISBN:978-0-9983486-3-6
Library of Congress Reg. No. Pending



Manufactured in the United States of America

Dedication

This book is dedicated to all the explorers discovering and uncovering the wonders of the Planet Earth and its moon.

## The A.T.E.

Sometimes people disappear but they don't just vanish into thin air. If anyone had said that to Sam three years ago she would have disagreed.

Now, her focus is on the current mission. She was the first selected to serve on Stoner's team. That gave her a sense of pride initially; but, she had stopped feeling grateful for her selection after working on Base 08 for the last two years.

The team for this mission are among the brightest and most creative on Earth. Although they were birthed and educated in three different countries, each shared a few essential characteristics. They were more than a little cocky, boldly honest, and fearless. They were also determined to succeed by overcoming any and every obstacle blocking their path.

These individuals knew that the mission would not be easy and that they were each sacrificing a lucrative career position to participate. Stoner presented the mission as a unique opportunity. "This is a once in a lifetime chance to be a part of something big," he told them. So big that it he said it was classified as "extreme secret."

Stoner disclosed the risks as much as he could, though the agreement each one of them signed specified the possibility of "unknown dangers." That didn't stop any one of them from signing on. Hell, a mission without some risk would have been a bit insulting to this group. They had, in their own ways, been trained to face challenges head on, and without hesitation. What would be the fun in completing a boring assignment? The reason they were recruited is because, in their respective area of expertise, they are the best of the best. In the past, performance success had always been expected of them because they were high achievers. Now, it was part of who they were. They were accustomed to the stresses of high performance expectations by others and their self-expectations were no different.

"An elite team" is the way they were described by Director Stoner. He also called them "a bunch of pansies" numerous times at the beginning of their training. When they came together as a team, showing a commitment to the success of their mission, he began to hum a different tune. During an early morning training review session, Griff (short for Griffins) changed Stoner's words to "a team elite" having the acronym A.T.E., the homophone for the number eight, which was coincidentally the number of specialists on the team formed by Stoner.

Sam thought the E letter should stand for eclectic because the eight of them together were the most unlikely bunch ever, like a group of people randomly selected by pulling cards out of a fish bowl at a business meet and greet. They would soon learn why they were hand picked by Stoner. He already knew the parts he would have each of them play in carrying out the mission.

Throughout their training, whenever one of them stumbled, no matter how slight, Griff would say that so and so nearly "ate it." Consequently, some of the team believed that was what Griff meant when he said, "No director, this isn't just an elite team, we are "the A.T.E.."

In the end, for whatever reason, this acronym reference for their team stuck and they began to refer to themselves collectively as the A.T.E..

Sam was amused because when she heard him refer to the A.T.E. she thought about his eating habits. Given the on-going physical training schedule they each endured it wasn't hard to believe that Griff could maintain a body-builder physique. However, after all the months of training that included their chores rotation for meal preparation, the A.T.E. learned that Griff had a weakness for sweets. If anyone could find a way to incorporate desert in each course of every meal it was Griff. Sure, they had three squares a day but the squares whenever Griff cooked were filled with an abundance of the type of foods they would not have access to once at their mission destination. They figured that Griff was only getting his fill of sweets while he still could. That may have been true; but, not the whole truth.

Griff was the brother Sam had once hoped for. Her relationship with each member on the team was good generally, but not a very close one. With Griff it was different. She sensed that there was a deeper understanding between them.

It was possible that this closeness stemmed from the fact that she had mentored him during his first month at the operations base where they were both previously stationed. They were in sync and Sam soon learned that she could trust his instincts.

During their first few months working together, Sam learned about Griff's culinary preference for donuts. She enjoyed teasing him about this by telling him that someday his metabolism would change and all the donuts he was eating would go right to his midsection. Griff would always reply the same way. "Good thing that day ain't today."

As it turned out, when Griff referred to the team as the A.T.E., he wasn't making a reference to either the team's learning curve or food. He was actually referring to the end goal of their mission. The goal was to establish the means for an alternative terrain evacuation.

Stoner would not at this preliminary stage in the mission disclose all its details. That was to be expected. Stoner was in the game long enough to avoid actions that might compromise the end goal of a mission. Notwithstanding, the seasoned team members knew how and when to read between the lines.

For the benefit of the two newbies, Griff pointed out what most of the team had already suspected. In Griff-like fashion, and under Stoner's disapproving look, he spelled it out plainly. "So we keep our focus forward and one eye on the prize that awaits us following this mission to establish an alternative terrain evacuation." As he spoke, Griff turned to face Matthew and James. The two nodded an acknowledgment. Message received. The others knew that Griff called each and every situation as he saw it, never sugar-coating anything (except the food he ate).

According to the Human Resources staff psychologist, Griff self-medicated with his favorite foods to help shed some of the emotional baggage that came with his rough start in life. Griff scoffed at that analysis; but if he had been asked, he would have acknowledged that he had suffered from childhood trauma.

## Griff

Following a year of living as a foster child after the sudden death of his parents caused by a drunk driver, ten year old Griff's residence with Scott and Susan Blake became permanent. The morning of the court hearing when the adoption petition was finalized started out as one Griff would not soon forget. Although the Blake's tried to keep the status of their petition a secret and the hearing a surprise, Griff knew something was up.

He had brought the mail in the day the Blakes received confirmation that the requisite investigation was complete and a hearing date set. Susan tried to lightly brush off the court mail by saying it was a summons to jury duty but Griff had heard his parent's groan when they previously had received a jury summons and Susan's reaction to this mail was way too happy.

The atmosphere around the house was always pretty good but after that mail came it got even better. Griff could feel it. He wasn't sure why, but the air in the household was lighter, as though some issue suddenly vanished, leaving behind a sense of peace and tranquility. Griff felt this way at school whenever he solved a problem that he had puzzled over for some time. At the moment of resolution, the build up of tension suddenly disappeared leaving a sense of balance in its wake. That's what he felt in the household now, balance. For Susan and Scott the feeling was one of relief, along with anticipatory excitement.

The morning of the court hearing Susan was up earlier than usual making a weekend breakfast and noticeably smiling more for no apparent reason.  After breakfast, she hurried everyone to get dressed quickly. She said that there was an important stop they had to make on the way to work.

Her dress made no sense either. The dress code for Fridays was always business casual at the college and she looked like she was going to church. She actually insisted that both Griff and Scott wear a tie. The last time Griff wore a tie (neck nooses he called them) was at his birth parent's funeral. Scott only wore one whenever he had an academic speaking engagement. They both knew it was pointless to argue with Susan so they put on the ties Susan had laid out for them and headed for the car.

On the drive, Susan thought about the whirlwind changes in their lives since the death of their friends and neighbors, the Starks. Scott and Susan had delayed starting a family in order to advance their academic careers and when they reached a time when becoming parents may have worked into their lives, they discovered their fertility challenge. Sure, there were option to consider, but, that all ended when tragedy befell their friends Karen and Doug Stark.

Scott and Susan were one of the few remaining constants in Griff's life after the loss of his parents. There was no other family member stepping forward to take care of him, which made them the best choice as foster parents. Susan and Scott saw this as a bitter sweet twist of fate, so without hesitation, they opened their home to Griff. They remained respectful of what they knew the Starks wanted for their son and intended to follow the plan for Griff that Karen and Doug had shared.

The Starks were well aware that their son was gifted. They watched in awe when he was able to take apart then reassemble a model rocket when he was three years old and at four years when he could replay simple tunes on the piano after hearing them for the first time. They agreed to have him tested while he was still in kindergarten.

Even though the tests were generally given to children after they entered elementary school, there was an exception made for Griff and he was tested at the tender age of five. Griff was off the charts in his results for both The Screening Assessment for Gifted Elementary School Students and the Stanford Binet (L-M). These results, along with those of other tests, set the first pavers in place for the path of which was to be Griff's accelerated education.

Scott and Susan Blake taught Physics and Calculus, respectively. They also headed the early college entry program at the main campus of the state university. Griff entered that program at the age of thirteen, following his state fair science exhibition entry win. The entry, a quantum displacement simulator, stirred the interest of the academic science community. Word spread fast following media coverage that went nation-wide. As a result, Griff began receiving invitations to visit colleges the likes of M.I.T. included, while most teens his age were, at best, taking on higher level math and science classes.

The Blakes were well aware that their foster son was gifted far beyond any of the best students they had mentored throughout their careers. They encouraged Griff to explore his talents,  while also maintaining his authenticity.

Other members of the A.T.E. were born and raised far from the libraries and lecture halls of academia.

## Matthew and James

Mathew and James were both raised in affluent Texan ranch families, descendants of the Old 300. Their families were among the original provided with land grants in Mexican Texas under Stephen F. Austin's first contract to colonize the area situated roughly 50 miles west of Houston. Though they were of British descent from those early colonists who had first settled in the Trans Appalachian South, their familial heritage culture was enriched over generations through social interactions with both Native Americans and Spaniards.

After a stellar performance in the MIT Physics graduate program, Matthew and James were brought into the space program by the same recruiter. The day they were affirmed into the program Matthew pulled James aside as he said with a wink "learn together." James immediately responded "burn together." It was the verbal exchange they first made at the start of their friendship in their first week at MIT and one they repeated throughout their studies.

It was no surprise that they were drawn to each other at MIT. While standing alone in one of the school's registration lines, Matthew overheard what sounded like friendly bantering among a few other new students. His attention turned toward the noise and he moved closer to get a better view of the student who was clearly the center of attention.

James stood tall among several students. He was holding what looked like a Stetson hat and registration packet in one hand and in the other, a pen that he held above his head while his attached arm moved in a wide circle. He was mimicking what appeared to be a cowboy twirling a lasso. As he drew closer Matthew could see the slight flick of the  young man's wrist and heard words matter-of-factly stated, like the period at the end of a sentence would read. "That fellas, is how it's done."

Matthew immediately identified with the young man who had the body-build of a cowboy that could only be achieved after many long sessions in a gym or through hard and rough ranch work. His bronzed skin and Texan accent suggested the latter. He recognized himself and couldn't resist the urge to have some fun. So he tapped the young man on the shoulder and asked him if he was hazing a tenderfoot. James smiled at hearing the Texan colloquialism and while turning to face Matthew he responded with a friendly "Howdy. No, I'm not trying to give these city boys a hard time, just showing them how to throw a lasso."

"So, what's a cowboy doing hanging round this ace-high establishment?" asked James. "Hoping I'm not barkin' at a knot," replied Matthew with a gleam in his eye. "Name's Mathew. Yours?"  "Yeah, same here. I'm James. Pleased to meet cha. Wanna sign up for classes together? It sure would be nice to learn with someone who looks like he can burn the oil as late as I can." "Learn together? Sure! I wouldn't mind burning the oil with a guy who looks and sounds like he's from my neck of the Texas range. I'm from East Houston. You signing up for physics 8.011 or 8.012?" A quick glance at Jame's registration sheet provided the answer so Matthew straightened his paper and circled Physics 8.012.

The two Texans became fast friends. That was no surprise, given their similar boyhood experiences. This commonality provided the basis for trust between them and for the thread they wove into a growing friendship based on mutual respect. Their understanding of each other was liken to that blood brothers growing up in the same household might have. When alone, they each put out an aura oozing of confidence and masculinity like a person ready to take on anything at any given moment. Together they were like the opposite sides of the same coin, each a compliment to the other. When problem solving together they demonstrated quantitative abilities the likes of which were described as incredible. “Isn’t it a crying shame we have to take all these boring intro classes before we can design and build robots?” asked James. “Yup” was Mathew’s only answer.

They were like two ears of corn on the same stalk. A genius stalk. They shared the same dormitory and classes so it made it easy to develop the same study schedule and recreation time. They even double dated only women who were approved by the other, trusting the opinion from the other who was, for that particular situation, rationally detached from the hormonal emotion and surging testosterone common in young men.

Matthew and James got on very well most of the time; but, there were times when the negative consequence of being close reared its ugly head and turned their normally quiet living space loud with an argument. These rare disputes never escalated physically, at least not as to blows aimed at each other. The Texans were well aware they each had a well fed ego and were willing to walk away knowing that sometimes it was just better to let it go. Though these rare occurrences were like Mexican standoffs, the one who started the argument usually ended it by saying he was headed to the campus gym for a workout. At the gym, they each found that blowing off steam on one of the hanging punch bags or by weight lifting was a much better option that throwing punches at each other.

During their studies at MIT they were both selected to participate in the undergraduate research and study program. The program offered through the Kavli Institute for Astrophysics and Space Research solidified a shared fascination of space exploration and robotics. They were destined to become space engineers but never forgot their Texas roots. They referred to themselves as "space cowboys" and successfully tackled every course challenge as a team, with the exception of the requisite thesis.

They met Stoner while attending a post-graduate aerospace robotics conference. Stoner wasted no time in recruiting them. They were unaware that Stoner had his eye on them and that he would have recruited them prior to their graduation, but he was preoccupied with a personal matter at the time.

## The O'Leary's

Finn and Ro O'Leary were the only members of the team who had studied at Oxford University. Griff referred to them as 'The Double Oxies'.

Born and raised in Dublin, Ireland, Finn and Ro were also the gingers on the team. Until the day they were born, the O'Learys thought they were having a set of twin boys and had agreed to name them Finn and Rowan in tribute to their paternal and maternal grandfathers. The birth of the twins went as expected, except that they did not have twin boys. After the surprise gender reveal and seeing their red-headed newborns, they decided to keep the names as planned. When Finn was eighteen months old his mother held Rowan on her lap and asked Finn who she was. Without hesitation the infant responded by saying "Ro." There it was. Although the nickname may have been inevitable, Finn was credited as the one who gave it to his fraternal twin.

Tragedy struck the O'Leary house when Finn O'Leary Senior died suddenly in a factory explosion. It seemed that a water pipe broke over a hot furnace causing an immediate explosive reaction that sent pieces of molten steel like projectiles across the factory floor. Finn senior was inspecting the line and just happened to be in the direct path of a steel bar that tore a hole the size of a basketball through his middle. The only saving grace was that his death was instantaneous. The phrase "never knew what hit him" echoed among the other plant worked and family friends and acquaintances.

Caring for her twins was the main thing that prevented Patricia O'Leary from slipping into a deep and dark depression. She was determined to raise the twins on her own and would have done so; but for the help of her older sister Claire who temporarily moved into their home two months after the funeral.

As the twins grew, so did their fascination with all things unknown. From an early age they analyzed every living (some not) thing they came across. Patricia O'Leary never got used to the surprises she uncovered when in the laundry room emptying the pockets of the clothing worn by the twins. It was a good bet that you could hear her cry out with what sounded like a mix of fear and excitement as she pulled something (or a part of it) out of a soiled pocket. Scolding them was of no use and besides, she was outwardly thrilled that they were curious children. Her own childhood had been constricted by a very strict mother who would have had a fit if she as much as came home with a smudge on her dress. Patricia reasoned that having Finn and Ro in her life was nature's way of correcting all the past wrongs she experienced in her younger days. She lived vicariously through all their adventures and at times was an active participant.

Until their senior cycle in secondary school the twin's education path intertwined as one. That changed during the last year of their senior cycle when Finn discovered that he had an interest in subjects related to human evolution and the effects of environmental interaction. His interest led him to pursue a degree in Human Sciences. Ro, on the other hand, remained passionate about practicing medicine.

Though it pained her to see them leave, Patricia beamed with pride when Finn and Ro were both accepted to study abroad at The University of Oxford. Finn began his journey to a become a Human Scientist with an Oxford University

Bachelor of Arts degree in Human Sciences and Ro began her three year pre-clinical component at Oxford's School of Medicine and Biomedical Sciences.

The twins returned to Dublin during school holidays and Summer breaks for the next few years. After Ro received her BA Honors degree in Medical Sciences she continued on to complete the clinical stage at Oxford; whereas Finn decided to further his education with a concentration in Psychology.

In his last year at Oxford Finn worked on several research projects, one of which was to be conducted in collaboration with a student from another university. His research team partner was a California native named Gretchen, who was studying at Stanford University in Stanford, California.

## Gretchen

Finn and Gretchen hit it off immediately. Their student working relationship blossomed quickly into a growing friendship. Before long, they began to spend more and more time on line together.

After just a few short months, the two began texting every day and night, sharing all the details of their days, from their eating habits to their choice of activities spent during their down time.

Gretchen had plans to continue her graduate study at Stanford and apply to Stanford's School of Humanities and Sciences Department of Psychology. She hoped that Finn would want to do the same. "We make such a great research team!" she exclaimed. Gretchen was right about that. Their research project on how cultural and societal changes can effect human development and evolution was highly praised by their mentors at both Oxford and Stanford.

Their paper was submitted to World Academics and subsequently selected for presentation at the International Conference in Psychological, Educational, Health and Social Sciences. That year, the Summer conference was to be held in Anaheim, California.

At the end of the semester Finn travelled across the pond to visit Stanford and meet with Gretchen to plan their conference presentation. Gretchen toured him throughout the Stanford campus, introducing him to several faculty members and a few of the administrative staff along the way. She was sure to include the Dean of Admissions for the School of Humanities and Sciences Department of

Psychology in the introductions and made a point of mentioning that she intended to coax Finn into applying at Stanford for his graduate studies. Finn smiled at that and at the slight wink in her eye he saw when she glanced his way.

The following week, Gretchen insisted that Finn accompany her south to the Pacific Palisades where her remaining family member, step brother Basque resided. "It's a great opportunity to show you more of California and besides I need some help lugging my stuff home for the Summer," she pleaded. "Yeah, well it's gonna cost ya. Us overseas movers don't come cheap," Finn answered.

Following a day of organized chaos, as Gretchen liked to call the end of semester packing, they readied her SUV for the road trip South.

## Ro's decision

In England, everything was going very well for Ro at Oxford. Her research project was focused on the variations of natural infectious disease immunity found in different world populations through genome wide association studies. She studied the origination of several infectious diseases and the effect that preventative medicine and treatment had upon its spread. While analyzing the data she had accumulated, she began to see patterns of similarity between a person's genome and their susceptibility to be afflicted with certain diseases. She also found that individuals within different population groups tested shared the same treatment success rate regardless of the variations in their native environment.

While conducting the clinical trials, Ro could see why the introduction of disease could ultimately become its prevention; but, there were many remaining questions.

Ro believed that understanding a patient's genetics was the key to developing the best preventative measures. The clinical studies available to her were limited in terms of the analysis conducted on prevention of a particular disease. Limited that is, aside from the data on the effect of the vaccines that were already developed and approved for the clinical trials. So, in her view, the approach to the research was somewhat backwards because the problem of prevention was already solved to a large degree. Her data basically confirmed the success rate various prevention methods had upon different population groups.

Ro was more passionate about her additional research on how the genome affected the rate of success. She wanted to identify a relationship between the genome and natural immunity certain people have to disease and how immunity could be duplicated in others who were vulnerable to infection.

She added a new layer to her research when she completed a comparison study on how sometimes variations in the genome complicated the disease spread. This project was the seed that cultivated her interest in concentrating her medical career on the prevention and treatment of infectious disease.

Soon after the clinical trial results were made public, Ro's data was widely sought after by other research facilities. This got her noticed.

During her residency at a research and development facility, Ro leapt at the opportunity to lead a clinical study research team chosen to study a Native American tribe. The tribe resided at Supai, located within the Unites States Grand Canyon National Park in Arizona. Ro was excited to make the change. After all these years spent inside labs and lecture halls, working on the ground with an unfamiliar population group would literally and figuratively be a breath of fresh air.

## Basque

Back in California, Gretchen and Finn proceeded down the coast slowly, stopping often to allow Finn time to soak in all the beauty of the California coastline.

They made a stop in Big Sur to hike through trails weaving around majestic redwoods dominating the landscape. Deciding to stay overnight, they "glamped" at a site with a breathtaking view of the Pacific. After enjoying a good dinner and one of the most spectacular sunsets Finn had ever seen, the two strolled along a nearby trail before heading back to their comfortable cabin for the night.

The next morning their ocean view was completely blocked by a thick fog that brought the temperature down to a chilly 50 degrees. "This is typical Cali coast weather. Sun then fog, with temperature swings as much as 20 degrees in the same day," schooled Gretchen.

"Once we get further south, it will be warmer, but along the coast it still cools down at night, even in the summer months. The summer sun shines hot and bright in Southern Cali. My step-brother Basque used to tease that he could see a "valley girl" coming from a mile away because of the sun reflecting off her oiled suntan lotion skin," Gretchen shared with a quick laugh. "I'll fill you in a bit about Basque." During the next and final leg of their trip, Gretchen did just that.

Basque's mother died when he was a baby. His father remarried ten years later. Five years after that, Gretchen was born. Basque raised her as his own after the passing of their parents, who were killed by a wrong way drunk driver when Gretchen was in middle school.

After a stellar performance in college, where he was a premed major, Basque went on to graduate school. It was in his first year there that he made the change in his career direction, from medicine to engineering. His hard work paid off when he was rewarded an advanced degree in project design and engineering.

While in his final year of studies, he was pursued by a top engineering firm to enter into a career in building project construction design. He declined to venture in that direction.

During a summer internship with a film studio, he had discovered that he had a talent working with special effects and costume design. Exercising his creative side appealed to him so much that he decided to seek a career path that would provide both an opportunity to use his education and give him a creative outlet. After graduation, he landed a position as a special effects artist/costume designer for a major film studio and never looked back.

Basque had easy access to special effects materials and became quite the prankster at home. During her adolescence and throughout high school, Basque delighted in scaring Gretchen by donning one of his head and masque creations. They were so realistic that Gretchen was afraid to enter the studio where he kept a sampling of the prototypes used in major studio productions. His eyes twinkled while he teased her by saying, “That’s one way to keep you out of my studio.”

Basque had been learning all about Finn ever since the start of his research project with Gretchen. She managed to weave something about him into the weekly video chats she and Basque had. While on their road trip south, Gretchen confessed as much to Finn. “It just breaks the ice early,” she explained. “Spoken like a true Psychologist,” Finn replied.

Finn suspected that Gretchen had been giving Basque information about him the same way she was providing him with background information about Basque. She shared numerous happy childhood memories of growing up under Basque’s watchful eye.

Her brother managed to make her feel less like an orphan and more like an important young lady. She was the only lady of the house and grew into the role with a sense of purpose and pride.

As they neared their destination, Finn realized how important the man he was about to meet had been in shaping Gretchen’s life. He admitted to himself and to Gretchen that he was a bit nervous.

As soon as Finn was greeted by Basque, any nerves he may have had were melted by the warm greeting he received. It was no surprise to either man when they became fast friends.

## Gretchen and Finn in California

Gretchen took Finn to all the famous places in Southern California. She especially enjoyed surprising Finn by not telling him in advance where they were going. Often times he could give a good guess of their destination by way of the direction they headed and a reference to the pocket map he had purchased or by looking at their location on a map application opened on his cell phone. They had lunch at Dukes in Malibu, spent an afternoon at the Getty Museum in Los Angeles, strolled around the Hollywood Walk of Fame, and ate a sunset dinner near the Santa Monica Pier.

Finn was totally blindsided when one early afternoon after having breakfast at a famous diner in a place called the Grove, they ended up stopping at a television studio. They waited in line for over an hour before being seated in the studio audience of a late night talk show. "Okay, I definitely didn't see this coming. Why are we here?" he asked. "Well, so you can see how people are interviewed and the audience reaction they get to what they say," Gretchen replied. "It's much more fun to see it in person than on television. Besides, there is likely to be a question and answer session after our presentation next month and this may help both of us. Mostly you though, considering I have some on camera experience." "Ah, yes that kid's show you appeared on…what was the name of it again?" Finn teased. "Hey! Nickelodeon was legit and I even made some bank doing it," Gretchen said while laughing. "Anyway, I promise you that this will be fun."

Their paper presentation at the Summer conference went seamlessly, as did the cheesy dinner theatre Gretchen arranged for Finn the evening beforehand. They ate roasted half chickens off pewter looking plates while entertained by knights on horseback doing a medieval show of jousting in the arena below. After their meal, they cheered for the knight colors matching their seated section while waving small flags bearing those colors. The show was actually very good, albeit a little silly at times.

After spending the Summer with Gretchen, Finn knew he didn't want to live without her in his life. The decision for him to apply to Stanford was made and the process started for a student visa.

A month before both Gretchen and Finn received notice that their applications had passed the initial review and they would be interviewed for admission, Gretchen travelled to Dublin to meet Patricia and Ro.

Patricia gushed with pride  when she saw how her son had clearly captured the heart of this beautiful and intelligent woman. She could see in an instant that her son's heart was also captured and for a brief second she felt a pang of worry for him.

His life was taking a turn in a direction unknown to him. Finn has always been so shy. Will he be able to handle the immense pressure and stress in store for him? Is he ready to be on a public stage under the spotlight? How will he handle being judged by his peers and by the haters who seem to enjoy any opportunity to ridicule someone on the rise? Don't get all caught up in nonsense she told herself. Instead, think of his success and allow yourself to feel only happiness for your son. Then the thought of future grandchildren flickered like the warm glow of fireflies in her mind. That's better, she thought. He will be just fine.

## The Havasupai

Supai is an isolated Indian Village inside the Grand Canyon. The village is located at the bottom of Havasu Canyon on the Havasupai Nation Reservation. The Supai tribe of only 600 is the smallest Indian Nation living in the canyon and have been there for at least 800 years. The tribe name means, "People of the blue green waters." The waters of the Havasu creek weave a vibrant turquoise throughout the canyon, creating several stunning waterfalls that accent the changes in elevation.

The tribe cultivates crops and weaves unique baskets; but, they mostly rely on the tourists who spend their money in the village businesses and to hike the trails leading to the spectacular waterfalls in the canyon.

Ro, her team, and all their gear, assessed the village by mule, one of only three ways in and out. When they were at the half way point they were all rethinking this choice, wishing they had opted for a helicopter instead. "But what would have been the adventure in that? At least we aren't hiking," Ro said aloud what the others were thinking. "We will definitely helicopter out when we are done here," she continued. The others nodded their agreement.

The group shared the same first impression of the village-It was like stepping back in time, a simpler time. The village had general stores, a post office, church, cafe, lodge, school, and other buildings that catered to tourists. It was like a town one would see in an old western movie, minus the wooden planked sidewalks.

After a good meal and settling in at the village lodge, the team turned in early for a well-needed night's sleep.

In the morning they met with the tribe elders to discuss the study plan that included obtaining the medical history of all 800 tribe members, complete with blood and tissue samples.

In addition to the monetary support the program provided to the tribe for their participation in the research project, Ro and her team were prepared to provide basic medical training and supplies. However, they quickly learned that the tribe elders were not all that interested in modern medicine. They intended to continue practicing the same holistic medicine as was practiced by their ancient ancestors. With that being the case, Ro and her team were the ones who received the medical training. Each of Ro's team saw this as a unique opportunity and eagerly accepted the elder's invitation to receive a crash course in ancient Havasupai medicine.

Before their instruction could begin, the elders assigned them to collect samples of certain plants growing along the hiking trails. They were also tasked with retrieving water samples from the water that formed the blue ponds underneath the falling waterfalls along those same trails.

For the next several weeks, Ro and her team documented the daily sessions of instruction. They manually kept handwritten records of the lessons in their journals. They also made audio and video recordings of each session.

At the end of an additional three weeks, the team had collected the medical history data and organic samples from all the members of the tribe.

Early on in that process, they noticed a trend in the medical history data. It seemed that the usual markers for common infectious illnesses was not found in the medical lineage history of the tribe members. What was even more astounding was that there seemed to be no record of the spread of certain illness within the random sampling reviewed. While tagging those samples for additional study, Ro was beginning to feel bad that she didn't ask for a longer field study time. This was turning into something much bigger and better than she had anticipated.

Two months earlier, Ro wasn't sure exactly what to expect because she was told that the request made to conduct the study on the tribe was the first such request ever made that was favorably considered. She wondered why this was, doubting that the reason was solely a financial one. After spending time with this tribe, who opened their village to a team of strangers that came to poke them for samples and prod them for their intricate medical history information, she was even more convinced that there was some other reason they were granted access for the study.

There was something mystical about the canyon and the Havasupai. Maybe she should just come right out and ask why they agreed to the study. Why not just ask, Ro thought. If there is some reason they believe that we shouldn't know they can make an excuse or simply refuse to answer. They have been pretty straightforward with us up to this point. If I don't ask we may never know. If I let this opportunity pass I know that the pain of regret will keep its grip on me for a long time. We have been open and respectful toward these people. Was that enough to gain their trust? Ro wasn't sure, but the one thing she was sure about was that they were running out of time.

One early evening while examining plant samples with one of the elders, Ro asked the translator to pose the question. The interpreter asked an elder named 'Ahaa Wilatause' (meaning water flower) while she was sampling one of the gathered flowers. She finished chewing the flower then drew in a deep breath. As she exhaled she smiled then moved to the circle around the fire and sat down. She sat still for several minutes, eyes staring intensely into the fire. When she finally spoke the interpreter jotted down her words in the notebook Ro gave her. When the elder stopped speaking the interpreter continued writing for several minutes before returning the notebook to Ro. Written neatly on the page titled 'yellow flowers' was the present date. Also written were notes stating where the flower was picked, how the flower was to be prepared, what holistic medicinal benefits it was believed to possess, along with examples of how the Havasupai used the flower.

Below this, the words written would prove to be one of the most difficult puzzles Ro had ever tried to solve:

> Ooo uuyu, nyeekumu, inyavum'be, makuinyame
> Musil uuyu
> Bami ginavo
> Hulaha Baku s'takume
> Thami yutuga
> Muvanyu wasjua Humuka-supe wilatause
> Hulaha hulawahyu
> Hane gawk
> Yatuga s'takume hulaha
> Opa nyaajavo ba
> Opa makuinyame
> Opa nyeekumu

Below that was the following translation:

I see [in] the fire, tomorrow, today, yesterday.
I see [a/the] girl.
Tell them all.
The moon is falling open.
Ready to enter.
You need eight flowers.
The moon is mooning.
It is good.
Enter the moon.
No sick man.
No yesterday.
No tomorrow.

Sure. Its all clear now, Ro thought. Clear as mud. "Any idea what that means exactly?" Ro asked the translator. The translator shrugged her shoulders and said, "Beats me, I just interpret the language not the meaning."
The cryptic answer brought even more questions to mind. They were nearing the end of their field time, so Ro just folded up the paper and stuffed it into her jacket pocket.

The night before their departure, Ro and her team were honored with a ceremonial feast. As she sat among the tribe circling the fire, Ro felt the warmth of friendship for the Havasupai people. Their calm demeanor was intoxicating. Ro sensed that the study would play an important role in the destiny of medical research. She felt privileged to sit among the Havasupai and knew that she would forever be grateful to them. She would later understand exactly how important their role would prove to be.

As their helicopter lifted off, Ro experienced mixed emotions. She felt satisfied with the team's accomplished project goals; but, she also felt sad that the field portion of the study was over and they were leaving these wonderful people. She would miss them and this magical place at the edge of the canyon.

## Holiday Celebration

The holiday season for Gretchen and Finn included the announcement of their marriage. Basque flew in for the holiday after Gretchen hinted strongly that he would not want to miss this year's family dinner in Dublin. Although neither Finn nor Gretchen thought it was necessary to marry before receiving their PhD's, they became aware of the benefits they would have as a couple, including better housing options. So, once their Stanford admissions were finalized, they decided to tie the knot privately while in Las Vegas for a weekend get-away.

"How simple was that?" Gretchen asked while unpacking her weekend bag back at Stanford. "Too simple if you ask me," replied Finn. "I feel like a rebel. Are you certain that counts? It just seems so weird that we could have been married legit by a guy under an Elvis wig. I was sure he was going to break out in a version of "Love Me Tender" at any moment." "Or "Jailhouse Rock" teased Gretchen. "That was why it was so perfect. We will always have just a hint of doubt to keep us on our toes and not take each other for granted." "Oh no, Mrs. O'Leary, I could never take you for granted. Come here and let me show you how I do means I do and I do." Finn pulled her close for a long deep kiss.

When she learned that her son had been married for more than two years, Patricia was a bit displeased, but also happy to welcome a second daughter into the family. She had suspected the couple had at least been secretly engaged because of the familiar and easy way they appeared together in video chats. They had the look of love for each other but also the look of lasting endurance seen in

married couples who could finish each others sentences or communicate with just a glance and a soft smile.
The couple promised that that would have a formal wedding ceremony and celebration when they had time to properly plan one. I won't hold my breath waiting for that Ro thought.

The holidays passed at a much needed slower pace for everyone except Basque, who was in the process of making final design revisions on costume head masks for a studio production that was scheduled to resume shooting in January.

This was, in and of itself, ridiculous, considering the upcoming award season schedule. What made things worse was that Basque was also nominated for an award. That, he thought, was both a blessing and a curse. He had a strong work ethic so of course his film commitment was paramount. However, he was aware that an award nomination also comes with responsibility. If he wins, the boost to his career could be substantial. As would be the demand of his time. Giving his best to both would require some tricky maneuvering on his part.

He wasn't usually presumptuous, but he couldn't help but think about winning the award. It would be his first. He had seen award acceptance speeches that were pre-recorded and acceptances by proxy so if he did win he was aware that he had options. Would he actually not appear though? Naw, he would be there. He already knew that much.

Basque was the first to admit that he wasn't very good at being diplomatic while under pressure. He called it like it was, good, bad, or something in between. For this situation he needed a buffer. So, he relied on a publicist for help with his appearance schedule and maintained his production deadline schedule himself.

He trusted his publicist's judgment so he tried to relax and let her do the job she was paid to do. Even with the extra support, he was beginning to show signs of stress.

Gretchen knew the minute she laid eyes on him. Her bother needed a diversion. "You, my best brother, need to take a load off and chill!" She handed him a tall glass filled with his favorite mixed drink, clinked hers into his and said, "Prost to you and to me and my hubby. Now, let's get you properly introduced to the rest of the family," she said with a wink.

Meeting Ro definitely took the edge off of Basque's heightened stress. Her easy going manner with him brought him to a good place where he was able to thoroughly enjoy himself.

He and the others listened with interest when she spoke about her medical research and the study of the Havasupai. Ro even shared the elder's cryptic message in hopes that maybe it would resonate with one of them. It did not; however, Basque shared that he read stories about western desert tribe culture and the use of peyote to enhance or trigger visions.

"Maybe that's what the elder is describing," he suggested. "Hmmm, that's an interesting possibility. One that I will dive further into for sure," Ro answered. "No more work diving please," Gretchen pleaded. "This is a celebration so let's celebrate!"

## Cat's out the bag

Three years later, Gretchen, Finn, Ro, and Basque attended a "People Against Drunk Driving" fundraising and awareness event sponsored by Stanford. While mingling among the crowd with Basque, Ro marveled at the irony of their shared family tragedies and how that common ground was something that would always provide a deep bond for all of them. "Our lives crossing paths the way they did makes me a true believer," Basque said. "Believer in what? I thought you were using this event as an excuse to spend more time with me," Ro hinted.

She and Basque had been steadily seeing each other since that holiday in Dublin. They were meeting discreetly so as not to draw attention from their families, meaning Patricia, who would not end the questioning, especially after what Finn and Gretchen did. In considering a serious relationship, there was more than the pains of Patricia that caused them pause.

Although it was rare for siblings to marry siblings, it was not unheard of. Their respective children would have the opposite grandparent lineage, maternal and paternal, but that only makes for interesting conversation. Their children would also be both cousins and either an aunt or uncle at the same time. Ro thought back to their conversation about that. Basque had said "Now that! That's a dinner conversation! The real question is, which came first, the cousin or the uncle?" "Or aunt?" Ro giggled. "Yup, we will just keep them going with that one." "There is just one thing I want to consider. How our interesting family tree may reflect upon my research of the genome. Our foundation has fierce competitors that could use our situation as an excuse to raise an eyebrow. If that happens it could disrupt the funding of our projects. If our funding stalls, we would be set back months on our data analysis. That would be tragic, especially because we are near to reaching the expected breakthroughs in our research.“ “So, you think that someone would be so egregious as to suggest that we would get married in order to provide you with a platform to advance your research? Wow! That makes even the Hollywood backstabbing seem like child’s play.“ “I would not be surprised by anything after what happened during the COVID 19 pandemic. People get crazy when big money is at stake. I just want to be very careful about our timing, that’s all. You know I love you more every day. A piece of paper is not going to change that.“ Ro lifted her head for a kiss that was promptly delivered. “Now, let’s find the bar. I could use a long cold drink.“

Basque led Ro toward a corner at the far end of the room where tiered rows of glass shelves holding various spirits could be seen like a glistening beacon oasis in an arid desert.

After taking a sip of their drinks Ro let out a sigh. With her back to the crowd she had spied familiar faces in the bar mirror. It was Gretchen and Finn and they were headed their way. “Aye! I should have known they would be here! Gretchen and Finn at 4:00 o’clock.”

“So, lookie who we have here darling. My lovely sis-in-law with big brother. Hmmmm how cozy! You forgot to mention you were coming here during our chat last week big bro. Why so secretive?” Basque was quick to answer with a lame attempt at evading her question completely. “Hey sis, how nice to see you too! Yes, well, er, it looks like great minds all think alike. Didn’t I mention that I was coming? It must've slipped my mind. Life has been pretty hectic lately and I,..." "What he means to say is that we were hoping to run into you here," Ro interrupted. "So, now you know and I for one am glad you do because all that sneaking around was getting old. Drinks are on us." Basque turned to order the drinks while the others shared their opinions on the conference.

With fresh drinks in hand. the four toasted to their families then turned their attention to the stage where an announcement was just made that the event key note speaker was about to take the stage. "Let's find a table Gretchen suggested."

## Griff makes an Introduction

The room was packed and most of the tables were already full. Ro pointed to the rear of the room at a table with only one person and said, "Let's ask to share that one." The others nodded in agreement as they made their way there.

Once everyone was seated, introductions were made all around. After the key note speech concluded along with the acknowledgment of patrons whose donations made the event possible, the crowd was informed that lunch service would begin soon. After the servers delivered their lunch plates, Griff excused himself to take a call while the others began munching on the chicken or fish entrees. During their meal they each shared their drunken driver stories.

Griff took the lead in that conversation upon his return to the table. "My name is Griff Stark. I lost my parents to a drunk driver when I was a boy." He went on to provide a brief synopsis of his life after the death of his parents, including his education and work history. The others followed in turn.

Griff knew the O'Leary's research, having read their published paper. They were like a well-oiled machine while discussing their behavior research in person. One of the two would begin with a hypothesis and the other would take over to describe how and why they had reached a particular conclusion. Stoner had given Griff specific instruction on obtaining their agreement to meet with him at a future date. Griff meeting Ro was an unexpected bonus. What luck! Even that tricky son of a bitch couldn't have predicted this! He respected Stoner but the way he was always one step ahead of everyone else could be annoying. He told himself that it was why Stoner got paid the big bucks, had access to the intel needed to pull off a tough mission, et cetera. But, Stoner had not thought of Ro. If he could get her to agree to a meeting he knew Stoner would definitely be impressed with her and with his initiative. Maybe then he wouldn't be so smug all the time.

Griff's feelings about Stoner were somewhat compromised because Griff still felt a bit put off by being overlooked as first in command on this mission in favor of Sam. Even though he had her to thank for mentoring him at the beginning, it was he who had taken the lead ever since. In fact he had taught her what she needed to learn about deep space signal recognition analysis. What Griff did not know was that Stoner had other information he held close to the vest and Sam was an intricate part of his plans.

When the lunch plates were cleared from their table, Griff said, "While what I shared with you is all true, that's not the only reason I'm here. Is there some place we can all talk in private? I would like to discuss your areas of research." Gretchen glanced around the table. She could see the look of surprise on the faces of the others. She herself was intrigued. As she stood, signaling her yes to the others, Gretchen said, "Follow me. We can use a staff conference room."

## A proposition

The five of them spent the next hour discussing cultural evolution and the affects that integrating different cultures can have on human behavior. They also discussed the ability of various cultural groups to quickly adapt to a sudden change in their living environment as documented historically in times of conflict and mass immigration.

Basque added another prospective to the conversation. He spoke from the point of view of a commercial artist. His observation of generational reaction to cultural change through the evolution of cinema added a multi-dimensional layer of thinking to the discussion.

Griff nodded his appreciation toward Basque then said that he had a confession to make. He revealed the true purpose of his meeting and how he had attended the conference in hopes of meeting them. “Truth is, I’m not the only one who was interested in meeting you. That call I took at lunch was from my boss, the Director of Operations for a NASA affiliated project. He wants to meet you and he is on his way to California.” “So, is your boss coming here to the campus?” asked Gretchen. “No, no, he’ll meet us at 7:00 for dinner at Morton’s Steak in San Jose.” Griff answered.

Not surprisingly, it turned out that Stoner was already familiar with the O’Leary’s research and had pre-arranged Griff’s chance meeting with them in Stanford. The surprise was that Finn’s sister Ro was with them. She had been on Stoner’s radar ever since he read about her progress in the area of studying native plants and Native American genealogy.

Until he took that phone call at lunch, Griff didn't think that Stoner knew Ro would be at the conference. Afterwards, he wasn't sure. Was Stoner tracking her? How did he discover that she was here? Did he have eyes on him? Griff was not at all shocked by that possibility, not in the least. He was sure of one thing. If Stoner wanted to meet someone and knew that someone would be at this conference, he would not miss the opportunity.

What a crafty bastard, thought Griff. He probably already knows more than I do. So, this is really a Stoner blind interview. He will no doubt use this as a way to initially vet them for our team.

Griff thought through the Stoner vetting approach he had become familiar with. He'll watch our interaction closely to see if there is any underlying personality clash that could surface later to disrupt the team goals. Sure, he'll ask me for my opinion and probably Sam too, but, in the end, if he thinks it can work, it won't matter much what either of us think.

Once Stoner decides on the team, the delegation begins. I will be charged with assuring that operations run smoothly from that point forward. That is acceptable. It comes with the job title-Tactical Operations Manager. Might as well be called the "pooper scooper" since any shit that happens will roll downhill to me. Again, acceptable.

Something else began to gnaw at Griff. Why wasn't Sam the one sent here to meet the Human Scientists? She was the first in charge of the team. Griff knew she trusted his opinion but team selection was definitely within her job description.

Stoner must have another card up his sleeve. I think that sometimes he hides information just to keep us on our toes, or to be a dick mused Griff. More likely that he does it just to show his superiority and that just pisses me off. As usual, I will keep that under my hat. As it turned out, Griff was not the only one on the team who felt that way about Stoner and his methodology.

## Sam, Steve, and Maddie

Sam believed that the mission would be her chance to reset her life to a time before she lost her grip on reality. A time before everything went haywire. She was not naive enough to believe that all her bad memories would be erased, but if she could get passed them somehow, it could make a difference in her life on so many levels. She knew that with the completion of a successful project there would be rewards. Maybe I'll finally get a transfer out of this shit hole and back to a base on top. Maybe I can salvage what's left of my marriage. That last thought? That one is probably asking too much. Sam sighed as she thought back on her relationship with her husband.

When she first met the man she married, Sam was of the opinion that the name Stephan was too formal and stuffy for a guy with such an easy going demeanor. After their first date she started calling her future husband Steve. No one aside from his mother ever used his given name and screw her anyway, thought Sam. She wasn't exactly the mother-in-law from hell but she was not a very nice person either. Steve's mother had a nasty short fuse. Her sick brain allowed her to spew insulting rapid fire sarcasm at anyone she targeted.

The first time Sam witnessed "the Helen tirade" as she referred to it, was when she and Steve got engaged to be married. At first she thought it was a joke when she heard Helen going on and on about how all her work in raising her son had come to this dreadful point. She soon found out it was no joke. Helen disapproved of their upcoming nuptials and made sure everyone at the engagement party knew it.

The last time Sam was on the receiving end of a Helen Mansion rant was the morning of their wedding rehearsal dinner, scheduled to take place on the eve of their wedding. Following tradition, Helen had arranged for the dinner that hosted the bridal party and several close friends. Because she was an alcoholic, Helen had insisted that nobody present consume alcohol at the event.

"Has she ever met anyone outside her AA meetings? It's okay by me that she doesn't drink but why does she think she has the right to control whether or not our friends can enjoy a glass of wine with dinner! I would just as well pay for the dinner ourselves rather than treat our guests like they are attending an AA meeting!" Sam was visibly angry.

"She likes everyone to feel her pain. She has been like this ever since I can remember." Steve took Sam in his arms and said, "Baby, relax." Sam asked, "Do you want me to try and reason with her?" Steve was quick to reply. "No. As infuriating as this is, I don't want to upset anyone before tonight. I'll simply give my own instructions to the wait staff and bartenders. They will serve drinks before dinner and keep the wine flowing throughout dinner. Helen is not going to ruin this." Sam smiled teasingly at her fiancé. "Oohhhh, I do like it when you assert yourself!"

By the time Steve's mother was aware of his instructional override, all their guests were enjoying drinks and appetizers. Once she noticed, Helen wasted no time before confronting Steve and Sam. "Just what do you think you are doing? I gave specific instructions! There was to be no drinking!" "Yes mother, and for you we hope that will be the case," Steve said as he led Sam away.

Sam recalled feeling a bit guilty when Helen passed away six months later. She must have known about her illness for quite sometime but chose to keep it secret. Always treat people kindly because you don't know what they may be suffering with, Sam reminded herself. I was kind to Helen, Sam thought. Steve and I tried to include her in our lives. Then she remembered the person Helen was and felt no remorse that they had grown distant of late. She was just mean and toxic. I have no regrets about not spending more time with her, Sam thought.

Sam's dislike of Helen Mansion wasn't the root cause of her current estrangement from Steve. I know that he blames me for losing Maddie. Sam felt an overwhelming sense of sadness as she thought about that dreadful day. He was right that I shouldn't have made an assumption. NEVER make assumptions about children! She's not even four years old! You stupid bitch! How could you lose sight of her? Those stinging words come back to haunt Sam more often than some of the beautiful memories she has of her only child. Some of those words originated only in her head, of that she was aware. Knowing how close Maddie was with her father was of no consolation either.

It was Steve who shortened her name from Madeline to Maddie. "Madeline is a name for a storybook girl, not a kid who, with us as parents, will be well grounded in reality," he said. Sam had to agree about that.

They named their only child Madeline after Sam's mother, who was named after her mother. Sam's given first name was also Madeline. If she were a boy, Sam would have been Madeline the III. When she was old enough, she dropped the name Madeline and referred to herself by a shortened version of her middle name Samantha-Sam.

## Madeline Hartwell

Sam's mother Madeline Hartwell was one of the first and longest lasting female engineers to bless NASA's space exploration program. Sam never knew her father; but, suspected that he and her mother were working colleagues. How else could she have met someone? She was a workaholic. It must have been someone she worked with all those long hours. Although she tried to get her mother to spill the beans about her father's identity on more than one occasion, it never happened. That must be because he was someone important, Sam reasoned in her young mind. So, throughout her adolescent years she created various scenarios about the private world her mother and father may have shared.

Sam thought that every man her mother introduced her to could possibly be her father. She played a little game of putting them into one of three categories: no way, maybe, and hopefully. Most of them went into the no way category. "First impressions are important!" Sam's best and only friend Lynne had told her that. Sam accepted most of Lynn's advice because she was a year older than Sam and had, as Lynne put it, "been to this or that rodeo before." Someday, I'll know the truth, Sam thought. As fate would have it, she would never learn the truth from her mother because Madeline Hartwell died a year after Maddie was born.

The timing of Maddie's first birthday party, held a month prior to her grandmother's death, could not have been better. The family was able to spend a carefree day of celebration together. There were three generations in the house at the same time celebrating life for the last time.

The memories from that very good day would be forever etched in Sam's mind. Whenever she thought about her mother, that day, Maddie's day, would be the first and finest of thoughts to come to mind. Those thoughts were like a gentle summer rain, warm and comforting. Her memory of that day helped soften the emotional blow that Sam felt after losing her mother.

Madeline was happy that day at Maddie's party. She clasped her gift to Maddie around Maddie's neck then unclasped the chain around her own and handed it to Sam. "I want you to have this and wear it now, while I can still enjoy seeing you wear it." The gift to Maddie, a gold chain with a hanging infinity symbol charm was exactly like the one Madeline wore, only smaller. She had worn that necklace as long as Sam could remember. Her mother never said as much, but Sam believed that the necklace may have been a gift from her father.

When Madeline first fell ill, she tried to give the necklace to Sam. At that time Sam refused it, saying that it was a morbid thing to do. Sam feared that her mother would not survive her cancer treatment until her child was born. After her birth, Maddie's presence seemed to spark a light inside her grandmother. Sam had not seen this side of her mother since her own childhood. Madeline stayed active in Maddie's life throughout her first year. She was present for all her only grandchild's first year of life milestones. Madeline lived in the house with Sam, Steve, and Maddie until the day came when her light suddenly went out.

When she died, Madeline left a legacy of achievements that would remain instrumental to the future success of the N.A.S.A (NASA) space exploration program. At Madeline's funeral service, Sam was astounded by all the references her mother's former colleagues made regarding her awards and achievements. Sam realized for the first time how low key and humble her mother was regarding her successful career.

The grieving process was new to Sam and not easy. There were days when she woke up with a light heart, only to feel a creeping sense of loss before noon. If not for Steve and Maddie, Sam would have had a much worse time of it.

Steve was the rock that kept their family on solid ground. As for Maddie, she was a source of continuous joy. She caused what Sam referred to as "combustion laughter" by her silly toddler antics. Although she had only known her grandmother for the first year of her life, Sam believed that the time Maddie spent with her helped to shape her in a positive way. "Never under estimate the power of a grandparent," Sam found herself saying to friends and colleagues.

Maddie reflected this sentiment in some manner or another from time to time and Sam would always notice. "When she makes that face, the uh huh face, she looks just like my mother. Oh, and did you see what she did this morning? If she had spent any more time with her I swear she would be a mini Madeline," Sam declared. "Yup. That's what grandparents do best," Steve replied in a matter-of-fact manner.

Madeline would remain an intricate part of their lives. She lived on with them in memory and would be instrumental to their future in a way they would later discover.

## Maddie and Steve

Maddie was a daddy's girl and began to demonstrate her preference for Steve over Sam before she could talk or walk.

Maddie's first words were "Ma dada." Steve attempted to ease any hurt Sam may have been feeling by saying that their child was actually saying ma (for mom) along with dada (for dad). Sam would not have it. "Oh yeah, right!" Sam laughed. "Naw, she's definitely saying my daddy, but that's okay because you can be the one to change her diaper as she clearly prefers you!" Steve was a good sport about that whenever his duty was called, "Just hand me a clothespin for my nose," he would say with a grin. Before long, Maddie got wise to this crack at her stink and one day brought one she found in the laundry room to Steve when she needed a change. Sam thought it was so funny that she put a small basket of clothespins by the bin containing fresh diapers.

After that, Steve started greeting Maddie by asking, "Who's daddy loves you baby?" Maddie always responded by saying, "ma dada," although her response became more refined, which is to say more understandable, as she grew.

Whenever the two were together, Steve would pick her up and twirl her around in the air. This would cause Maddie to yelp with delight as she went totally limp in his arms. This display of trust only strengthened the bond between them.

In contrast, Maddie was affectionate toward Sam, but usually greeted her by asking for food or expressing displeasure about something. Sam didn't mind because she knew well that she was instrumental in providing for her daughter's health and well-being. Sam was secure in her relationship with Steve and his relationship with Maddie brought her great joy. Taking care of the two of them gave her a strong sense of purpose and that was her anchor.

## Maddie Disappears

The day Maddie went missing was the first time Sam felt distant from her husband. As a couple, they never fought, not really. There was the occasional stand off over decisions they made that involved the farm or their daughter. That was normal, Sam thought. All couples disagree at times. The arguments never lasted more than half a day and always ended with good sex. Sometimes it seemed as though one of them would pick a fight just for the sex at the end and that became a source of playful banter between them. The arguments turned into spats over stupid things like what take out food to order or which movie to watch. They had a deep connection the likes of which make for a lasting partnership.

Steve was not playing now though. This was no game. What was happening now felt like the world crashing down around her. Sam was taken by surprise and rendered too disabled by worry to think straight.

She stood in the field while the sun slipped low to the horizon and the light of day changed to twilight. She just stood there like a scarecrow with a terrified expression on her face, her voice all ready hoarse from calling Maddie's name over and over, again and again. The sound of Maddie's scream echoed in her head and the hours that past since the morning seemed to have passed in slow motion.

Sam had been gardening at the end of a lazy, perfect morning. A morning that began like most Sundays, with the sounds and smells of bacon frying on the stovetop, pancakes cooking on the griddle, and a fresh pot of coffee brewing. Maddie had asked for blueberry pancakes and Sam obliged. When Steve entered through the archway that separated the kitchen from the dining room, Maddie was standing on a stool in front of the griddle dropping blueberries into the gooey pancake mix Sam had poured. She turned to see her daddy and said "I am putting extra burberry for you dada."

At nearly four years old Maddie had mastered sounding out 'bl', but after her parents laughed the first time she mispronounced it, she deliberately repeated the incorrect pronunciation whenever possible just to make them laugh. Sam tried to keep a list of all the mispronounced words and phrases Maddie uttered, knowing that someday recounting them would be fun. She remembered making a mental note of this one. Burberry is blueberry.

Steve had gone out to the barn after breakfast, leaving Sam and Maddie in the vegetable garden fifty yards from the side porch of their house. Sam heard the sound of the telephone ring through the kitchen screen door, stood up and walked toward the house.

The call was from Stoner, her boss and the Director of Project Operations. He rarely called on a Sunday, but she knew that if something urgent arose, her day could be interrupted. On Friday, Stoner had said something about meeting in Washington regarding preparations for a new project. Sam wondered if Stoner would ask her to go in to their base operations facility to retrieve a file or document. He's always forgetting paperwork Sam thought. It's a wonder he remembers his travel documents. Then Sam recalled the time Stoner forgot those and she had to make a last minute run to the Phoenix Airport. So stressful! At least I'm not with him. He can be a real pain in the ass.

Stoner sounded different this time. His voice had a heightened urgency quality to it that Sam had not heard before. "Change of plans Sam. I'm in the desert securing a classified crash site. Meet with Griff tomorrow and stand by for instruction." That was it. He sounded like someone out of breath from running but who had just stopped briefly in the middle of the race to make a phone call. Weird, thought Sam. So he didn't go to Washington. I should be used to it by now. Stoner calls and tells me jack squat leaving me to wonder until he decides to fill me in at some future point in time.

Not more than a few minutes had passed before Sam returned to the garden. Maddie was nowhere in sight. Sam began to walk around to the front of the house thinking that maybe Maddie had wandered there. She reached the front porch. There was still no sign of Maddie. Sam quickly circled the rest of the house, ending up back near the garden. That was when she heard the scream.

Maddie's scream came from the direction of the corn field beneath the meadow that was their backyard. When Sam heard the scream she instantly knew something terrible was happening. Her scream was a high-pitched, shrill sound that only young children can make. Sam had only heard that scream one other time.

About six months ago when the three of them were in the barn, one of the pitch forks used to pull hay from the upper birth into the stalls underneath had somehow come loose above their heads. Maddie was looking up when the sharp pronged fork started to fall, with a trajectory that put it landing directly on the top of  Steve's head. At that instant Maddie let out a scream so shrill and loud that both Steve and Sam jolted sideways. The fork had missed Steve's head; but, its end prong punctured the edge of his left shoulder. He called Maddie his little hero after that. Sam tried to make light of it for Maddie's sake, teasing that Steve would do anything to get out of the farm chores for a couple of weeks. Truth is, Sam would look back on that day and wonder if the pitch fork falling was not some kind of omen, one that perhaps she should not have ignored.

Sam felt her heart racing as her adrenaline soared. She stepped forward without looking at the ground and found herself tripping over a box of garden stakes she had planned to put in a tomato plant row. As she regained her footing, she let out a moaning sound as if someone had just sucker punched her in the gut. Then she ran. She ran so fast that her feet barely touched the ground. She ran as though she was being chased by evil. When she talked about that moment later, Sam would say that while she ran, she thought about evil. She thought that her baby girl must have come face to face with something evil. Only something dangerously evil would make her scream like that. As she ran toward the corn field Sam felt strong and brave enough to fight anything or anyone evil that had caused her Maddie to scream that scream.

Steve was exercising one of the horses in the lower acreage when he heard Maddie's scream. He was already dismounting Italian, his favorite stallion, when Sam closed in on the field.

"What the hell Sam! What's going on?" "I don't know! I heard Maddie scream and came running! I assumed she was with you. She was in the garden with me when the phone rang, but wasn't there when I came back out. I was only gone for a few minutes. She couldn't have gone far. I looked around the yard but couldn't find her. I thought that maybe she had wandered your way... she knew that you had gone to tend the horses . . . and . . . Oh God where is she? Maddie! Maddie! Where are you! This is not a game Madeline! Madeline Lillian Mansion -You come out right now!" "Do you really think yelling at her like that is going to make her come out if she's hiding Sam?" The tears were flowing down her cheeks and her throat tightened, causing Sam's voice to crack as she continued to call Maddie's name.

Steve had his phone pulled from his saddle pouch and had his arm extended upward trying to get a strong enough signal to make a 911 call. He remounted Italian and rode off only turning back once to shout instruction over his shoulder for Sam to stay in the field and keep looking for Maddie. He was going for help.

With a quick kick to the horse and a loud "Yah" he was gone, leaving Sam crying in the field still calling Maddie's name between sobs.

## The Search for Maddie

An all out search was launched that lasted several months; but, Maddie was never found. At the beginning, all law enforcement focus was on Steve and Sam. They were the last persons known to see Maddie alive and were naturally suspects. The interrogation was intense and cruel, but necessary, or so they were told. Their house was searched several times with the contents strewn about. Their personal laptops were seized. As upsetting as this was for the two of them, Sam and Steve remained a united front at the start of the process. Steve had to hold Sam back when they searched Maddie's room. "Don't you touch any of her things!" Sam shouted from the hallway outside Maddie's room.

After the search team left their home the first time, Sam looked for the stuffy that Maddie usually slept with. The small dog was a gift from an anonymous work colleague of her mother's and she couldn't remember if Maddie had it with her in the garden the morning she disappeared. She carried her "doggie" everywhere but Sam could not remember. She started to look around Maddie's room for it when Steve came to the door. "Babe, come on to bed. You must be exhausted." "Have you seen Maddie's "doggie?" I can't remember if she had it with her when she was in the garden and it's not here. She won't be able to sleep without it, oh Steve!" Sam started to softly cry. "If it's not here and wasn't outside, she must have it." Steve offered the words he hoped would comfort her, then pulled her close to hold her while she wept.

During the first few weeks after Maddie's disappearance, Sam would sit in her room at her usual bedtime with her blanket in her lap burying her head in it for comfort. She was glad she had neglected the laundry the weekend Maddie disappeared because the blanket still had Maddie's scent. It was this blanket the police used to give Maddie's scent to the search dogs that combed their property and the woods beyond.

Sam stayed in the chair next to Maddie's bed until she fell asleep. Sometimes she dreamed Maddie was there in her bed just like she used to be after her bedtime story. A dark shadow of sadness greeted Sam when she woke up to the continued nightmare that was now her reality. Her child was missing and there was little she could do but worry.

The investigation process wasn't good for her marriage either. It included separating her from Steve during their interviews. They were each advised to retain separate legal counsel. So much for a united front, Sam thought. She understood why having separate counsel was necessary since neither of them could swear truth as to the exact whereabouts of the other when Maddie disappeared.Still, it seemed as though they were each baited to stand against the other.

Maddie's disappearance was covered by news stations around the country and by the international press. Stories went viral on social media sites. At first, there were tips called in daily by people in numerous states and a few across the borders of both Mexico and Canada from people saying that they saw Maddie. Each one of these tips was followed as a separate lead and each one dismissed for one reason or another. After a few months, the tips stopped coming in. Sleuths on social media helped to keep interest in the case alive for awhile longer. Although the matter remained an open missing person case, without any new leads, it began to run cold.

As if that were not enough pain for Sam and Steve to handle, there was some talk of child neglect by a social worker from Children's and Youth Services. Since Maddie was never in their system, there was not much they could do except perhaps muddy the waters. Once Maddie was found, it would be determined if their intervention was warranted. It was just so incredulous to everyone hearing the news about Maddie, that a four year old could vanish from her own property without any trace.

In the end, there were no charges brought against either Sam or Steve in the disappearance of Maddie. This was because there was no evidence to support foul play of any kind.

One may suggest that the fact that a child is missing should be enough to infer foul play is afoot. That sentiment was echoed among some people who had seen a newscast covering the story. Others offered possible scenarios of what could have happened to the child. There were even a few psychics who came forward with their own theories. They offered no comfort to Steve and Sam. How could visions of your child being abducted by aliens, trafficked by some underworld organization, or being held by a stranger be helpful?

## Separation

In spite of the support they had for each other, Maddie's disappearance took its toll on Sam and Steve's marriage. After the first anniversary of the tragic event arrived and passed with no real break in the case, Steve moved out of their house and into a hotel in town.

The couple still saw each other on occasion; but, a barrier had formed between them. It was the type of wall people put up to protect themselves from an avalanche of heartbreak they believe they would surely feel if they were to try and live happily together while their child remained missing. The deep connection Sam and Steve once had was broken by the loss of their daughter. Even while living apart, they felt a profound sense of helplessness whenever they spent time together. For the time being, they both knew it was best to live separately.

Shortly after their separation, Steve was off to Marshall Space Flight Center in Redstone Arsenal, Alabama to contribute his expertise for developing the testing protocol of new compulsion system technology. Steve was a quality system engineer at the launch center, and could identify a compulsion system issue faster and more accurately than anyone else in his field. The change to to Marshall offered him a break from the tragedy that was beyond his ability to understand or fix- Maddie's disappearance.

Sam stayed at the Houston space center utilizing her Astrophysics education from MIT Kavli Institute Radio Astronomy. After mentoring a new staff member, the teacher became the student when she received specialized training in identifying and interpreting deep space signal data. The data was downloaded onto a secure server by volunteer enthusiasts all over the world.

Steve and Sam stayed separated; but, neither of them took the next step to a divorce or to sell the farm. They both shared a hope that Maddie would someday return to the farm. If she did return, they wanted her to find everything there just as it was the day she disappeared.

Although they lived apart, they left the imprint of their marriage visible on the mail received at the farm address. All of the correspondence from their joint bank and credit accounts was still addressed to Mr. And Mrs. Mansion.

After leaving their farm in the hands of the caretakers they hired, they each turned to their work for some distraction from the deep and dark sorrow that laid heavy in their hearts.

## Base 08

Sam's occupation with work was a good thing, at least at the beginning. She was a stellar employee, but that changed after losing Maddie. This tragedy, along with watching her marriage fall apart, was soon reflected in the decline of her mental and emotional stability. She began to lose her ability to concentrate on work and subsequently slipped into depression.

Social media became an obsession with Sam. She spent hours each day scrolling through hundreds of pictures she found on web pages while searching for girl children who may look like she thought Maddie would have aged to look like. She had read that children rarely remember much about their childhood before reaching the age of three. But Maddie was almost four when she disappeared so she could remember something, right? She would remember Steve and me and the farm, right?

Over the next year her work at the center suffered as Sam continued to lose focus. After a couple of write ups and an in person sit down with the base commander, Lieutenant Samantha Mansion received notice of her transfer to Base 08, an underground outpost with no access to social media.

Recruitment to work at the base was highly selective, or so Sam was told. The process started with a background determination check that included information on every job and club association the applicant had. Juvenile delinquency matters disqualified the candidate. The papers on each candidate were analyzed and if the individual passed, they had interviews. There were usually one or two by a five member panel, followed by a final, in person interview with the Personnel Officer. Sam was able to bypass the vetting process for Base 08 because she worked for Stoner and he seemed to have an unlimited reach when it came to decisions made in his favor.

At first and until she regained her grip on reality, the only internet Sam had access to during work hours was a classified connection to data files she was tasked to interpret. She spent the days and sometimes nights doing nothing but listening to radio signals from deep space, interpreting what she heard, and plotting the signal's origin on a map if she was able to confirm at least a 76 percent probability of authenticity. Sam documented her findings in bi-weekly summary reports that were sent to Stoner via a secured i cloud link.

The base was not too far from the farm, so Sam could have ventured home on weekends, but the memories there were still too fresh, so she opted not to. The caretakers Steve hired were working out, so there was no need to go there anyway.

Base 08 had barrack type accommodations, but her officer status provided that Sam was assigned a private two room suite with a bath. It was a bit rough, but enough.

She spent her after work hours at the base taking advantage of the recreation facilities. If the weather was nice she went ATV off-roading with a few of her colleagues. Whenever she wanted to be alone, she explored the web of passageways that hugged the parameters on each base level.

Through these corridors one could go from one end of a level to the other without the need to weave through that level's obstacle course layout or run into other personnel. Sam recalled entering the base on her first day and how she marveled at the feat of engineering which would have been required to build such a place.

The base entrance was quiet, but for the faint sound of music playing in the guard stations and a continuous low pitched humming sound that could be heard in the background. The hum was like a heartbeat, ever present, but something barely noticeable unless you purposely listened for it. Sam thought the hum was likely caused by the air ventilation and cooling systems. After her first few days and nights at the base, she could no longer hear it.

The base entrance tunneled into the side of a small mountain. The entrance provided access to the base on its ground floor Level 01(L1). It was impressive, especially considering that it was carved out of a solid land mass. The entrance was wide enough to accommodate several semi trucks driving in side by side, but it was limited by design to two lanes divided by a twelve foot wide median and walkway paths on either side.

The delivery trucks were directed to the left and a stop at the guard station and scanner located twenty five yards past the mouth of the cave-like entrance. The scanning equipment was similar to that commonly used at truck weigh stations found along interstate highways. Once at the scanner, a gate arm dropped down and remained down until the truck was scanned. A bar that protruded from the equipment like the wand used to scan people at airport checkpoints raised to a height two feet taller than the truck then slid over the top and down the other side. Another bar slid out and under the length of the truck to scan underneath. The whole process took less than five minutes.

Following the scan, the guard operated the gate lift upward to allow the truck driver passage.  Soon the guard could see the illumination from the truck's rear tail lights disappear down into the tunnel. After unloading at the far end of the base, the truck driver was directed to a turn around and to drive back out of the same entrance on the opposite lane.

All other traffic entering the base was directed to the right and into a parking lot. Beyond the lot was another guard station with an imaging and metal detector. Further past that there was a row of five elevators along the right tunnel wall. The first three were for passengers, the fourth for freight, and the last large enough to carry a vehicle. All were accessible with a passkey that worked to unlock the call and floor buttons.

About ten yards ahead of the elevators there was another narrower tunnel. This tunnel  was used by base personnel to travel straight back into the base on this the delivery and transport level. The other ten levels on the base were subterranean.

The base medical facility offices and hospital was on L2, as was the chapel. L3 through L7 were used for base personnel living quarters. The cafeteria, commissary, and break rooms were on L8. There was also a small gym with adjoining locker rooms and a heated pool and sauna. The theatre room had enough seating to accommodate twenty-five viewers. At one end of this level you could find an entertainment area with billiard and ping pong tables. A separate arcade contained old school pinball and video game machines.

L9 and L10 were filled with offices and working labs.

The base level deepest underground required the highest security clearance. Level 11 (L11) was inaccessible without a clearance so secret it wasn't even specified as a category on the security level chart. The classification for L11 was identified solely by the infinity symbol that could be seen on the inside of the elevator doors. Although there were rumors circulating about the happenings on L11, no one not privileged to work there ever dove into those deep waters because L11 did not officially exist.

At least not as far as the general public was concerned. Staffing at the base was limited due to budget constraints and this worked well to mitigate employee turnover. It did not, however stop the employees from gaining access to or knowledge about the projects on L11. If you worked at the base for any length of time, there was a good chance that sooner or later you would be required to spend some time on L11.

An attempt thwart employees from leaking classified information about L11 was made a part of the on-boarding process. All new hires signed a non-disclosure agreement regarding L11 that included serious legal consequences. This wasn't a great security measure, but one that should give an employee pause before that individual decided to leak classified information to the public.

There were several ways to access L11, but the access details were not provided to most of the base workers. One way was through one of the doors located at regular intervals along the outer corridor of L10. These doors each opened up to stairwells that led down to the maze of tunnels around and under L11.

There was also the freight elevator that would not stop on L11 without inserting a passkey. This large freight elevator was 40 feet long, 25 feet wide and 15 feet high, large enough to accommodate a small airplane.

The freight elevator rear door was programmed to respond only if the proper security code was entered once the elevator door closed on L11. Exiting through the rear freight elevator door was the only base exit wide enough to accommodate a trailer or truck with cargo and was the only exit considered completely secure and discreet. After the door code was entered and the rear door unlocked, the heavy door panel would begin to slide sideways. Once this process started, it was impossible to stop or to reopen the front door.

The outside of the massive door was camouflaged with a faux layer that gave it the appearance of a mountainside in its natural form. The surface was covered by natural plant growth in places and blended in nicely with the surrounding mountain, even when viewed from a short distance.

This rear exit was monitored by guards stationed inside and at the rear of L11. Their daily activity logs and videos retained the details of all activity occurring from the time the code was entered to open the door to the time of the door closing.

While walking in the outer corridor on L10 during a lunch break, Sam saw a door in the wall that she had not noticed before. At first she thought it may have been an equipment room, perhaps housing the computer system for L10.

Some weeks later, when she was walking past the same door, she noticed it was slightly ajar so she stopped to take a peak at what was inside. The light from the corridor flooded past the open door to illuminate a descending stairwell. Hmmm, this must be one of the entrances to L11 that I have heard about, she thought. Sam checked to see if the door would lock if she closed it and found to her surprise that her key card provided her access. This was definitely not on my orientation tour she thought and she wondered why Stoner never mentioned it.

Sam pushed the door open wide then quickly walked down the stairwell two flights to the bottom. Once there, she found herself standing in a hallway that a forked about twenty or twenty five yards ahead. Sam decided to go right and found herself at the beginning of what appeared to be a tunnel maze. Okay, this looks complicated. I could get lost fast in here she thought. At minimum, I'll need a flashlight, or at least my cellphone. Sam made a mental note of what she had seen so far then headed back up to her office on L10.

## Hidden stairway

On February 14th of her second year at Base 08, Sam was on a work break and jogging in the surround corridor on L10. She had left her office to stretch her legs and release the tension that this lover's holiday brought. Being single on Valentines Day sucks the big weenie she thought when she woke up alone. She had to admit that the day wasn't really going that badly. She had received gifts from Steve and that cheered her up a bit. Considering their current separation status, she thought that he had gone above and beyond any expectations she could have had. After eating a half pound of Belgian Chocolates, Sam stopped working and sat still, just looking blankly at the floral arrangement on her desk. It may have been the sugar speaking to her but she suddenly snapped out of her daze and had the urge to run.

After two laps around L10, she decided to explore the tunnel maze on L11. This time she stopped back at her office for a small backpack that held her cellphone, a headlamp, water, and a couple of energy bars. Just in case, she thought. It never hurts to be prepared. Her knowledge about the tunnels was limited; but, she had heard that they were sometimes used to discreetly usher unofficial visitors on and off the base.

At the fork where the tunnels split, Sam spied several open cart vehicles parked along the wall. She hopped on the first one she came to, turned the key, and drove it into the tunnel farthest to her right. As she headed in what she thought was a westerly direction, her mind wandered. These tunnels are like the root system of a tree.

That thought triggered a memory she had of a vacation trip to Big Sur. She was hiking with Steve along a trail that threaded its way between the giant redwoods that area of the coast was well known for when he suddenly stopped, turned to face her, then repeated a paradox her mother told her when she was a child. “If a tree falls in the forest and no one is there to see it does it make a sound?” Sam had puzzled over that for a couple of days before casually telling her mother that she knew the answer. When her mother asked her what it was, a ten year old Sam looked at her squarely and said, “Yes, the tree makes a sound for anyone who’s there listening.” The day with Steve in Big Sur she just laughed when she answered the question by saying, “Yes, it makes a sound as loud as the light is bright from the photon that no one is watching.” Sam found herself smiling while she lingered in the memory.

As she.made her way deeper into the tunnel, Sam’s phone kept track of the distance and exactly at 220 yards she found a cutout with a door in the right tunnel wall. The door was marked with the Letter A and the number 01/8. This looks like a mile marker you see along the freeway, only it’s an eighth mile marker. Her cell phone confirmed the distance. So this must be Tunnel A at the eighth mile mark. Sam tried her key card in the door lock without luck so she got back in the cart and pressed on until her cell phone indicated she had gone into the tunnel nearly a half mile.

Suddenly she heard the faint whirring sound of other carts headed in her direction. She slowed her cart to a stop and waited. Well, that’s it. I’m about to be busted. Her mind raced with ideas for what she could give as an excuse for being in the tunnels. There was no need. A caravan of carts driven by base guards drove right past her without as much as slowing down. Sam could see that each cart had two guards, a driver, and another passenger not in uniform. I wonder if they are the special guests I've heard about? After the carts past, Sam stepped out of her cart and went to the wall. Sure enough, there was a cutout with a door marked with the letter A followed by the number 01/2. This time when Sam tried her pass card she heard the soft click as the door unlocked. She found a set of ascending stairs with twelve step intervals and decided to climb.

Sam thought that this stairway might be an emergency exit from the tunnel. The fact that she had not been advised of that during her orientation entered her mind as a reminder that her presence was unauthorized. She dismissed the thought, justifying her trespass as scientific research. She kept count of the number of flights and noted that at each interval platform there was a plaque on the wall with a minus sign followed by a number. The numbers were sequential in ascending order. Sam calculated that since she started out on L10 and had descended two levels to the tunnel she should have been on L11 when she began to climb; but, instead, the first wall plaque she came across after walking up two flights was marked with a minus sign and the number 10. The tunnel must gradually slope downward she reasoned. She counted the flight of stairs to a point where the plaque read 0. Okay, so this must be ground level.

She pressed on, now surely climbing above ground because the plaque numbers were steadily increasing. Sam lifted her head up and back to see the stairwell. She wasn't sure how much farther it went. Thoughts were racing in her mind. Where is this leading? She didn't have to wait long before finding out when she reached the small platform under a wall plaque that read +7. So she just climbed nearly a twenty story building? That's insane.

She wanted to open the the door but there was no handle. There was nothing but the smooth surface of the outline of a door. In the wall next to the door Sam saw a keypad without numbers or letters. Instead, there was the infinity symbol and a grooved indentation. On a whim, she held her keycard over the area but the door would not open.

Great. She also fit her forefinger into the grooved indentation but that didn't work either. After all that and it stops here she thought. Why would my keycard open the door to the stairway if I don't have the key to open this door? Feeling somewhat defeated, she turned around and found her way back to her office.

Well isn't that just peachy! Now I'll be working late while being frustrated. My legs are gonna feel this too! Then, as usual, she looked for the bright side of the situation. At least I got in a good early workout.

When she reached her office Sam began to pace the floor. Maybe I should call Stoner right now and demand some answers. Sam went over her prior briefing with Stoner.

He told her about the Order, the overseer of NASA, the earth's international space programs, and the international space stations. Sam learned that this was the organization she had really been inducted into by Stoner following the death of her mother.

He had told her the Order's goal for the signal analysis when she was first transferred to Base 08. He told her that the PCb Federation was coming to negotiate an agreement with the Earth's Order for their use of the moon base in exchange for the advanced technological knowledge needed to reopen the portal on the moon. He said that if the portal could be reopened, that might provide the human race with an alternate evacuation route from the moon base to another inhabitable planet.

Sam knew that this was only part of the whole truth. The part that Stoner chose to tell her. He was always coy about the details of missions he had a hand in. If you worked under Stoner you knew that he fed nuggets of information to his direct reports and not the same nuggets to each. So, it was a good bet that he never provided any one person with all the information he had.

Stoner believed that his staff need only know what he deemed sufficient. Yeah, the "need to know." What a crock of bullshit that was. As if the people who risked everything should be kept in the dark about something that could save or take their lives. The truth was, the "need to know" was only a level of security used to delay someone from jumping the gun in a sensitive situation.

Anyone with a security clearance knows that there are some highly educated and skilled, albeit twitchy, individuals who work among the ranks of special task teams. You have to be a little crazy to be in that line of work. A little crazy was okay with Stoner, as long as the mission objectives were met without unnecessary casualties. Now, I'm wandering Sam stopped pacing.

Why do I always go down a rabbit hole whenever I analyze Stoner? Sam grimaced. It must be because he is so damned annoying! How did my mother stand to be around him for so long?

Sam learned many things from her mother, the most important being that she should always question a situation that smelled the stench of deception. Sam smelled that stink now. Something was off but she couldn't quite put her finger on it. She felt sure that Stoner was up to something. But, she knew that it wouldn't do her any good to poke around for answers.

For now, her focus must stay on the task at hand-to locate, identify, and analyze a signal that could be confirmation of a spacecraft heading their way.

She sat down at her desk and slid her computer mouse across its pad to wake up the computer. She made a mental note to ask Stoner about the stairwell. She obviously had authorization to access that part of the base, so why hasn't he said anything? She shook her head, popped another chocolate into her mouth, put on her headset, and turned to her computer.

March 19, 2040

Four weeks later, on the third Monday of March, Sam decided to begin her work day earlier than usual. For the previous consecutive seven days she had been analyzing a series of transmitted signals that followed a repeated pattern. This was quite extraordinary, especially considering that the origin was mapped to Proxima Centauri b (PCb). PCb is an exoplanet orbiting Proxima Centauri, a red dwarf in the Alpha Centauri system, which is located in the Centaurus Constellation.

These signals were especially exciting was because PCb had been identified as an exoplanet that is possibly inhabitable. Therefore, it was possibly inhabited. There was also something else.

The origin of the transmission was the same as that of a similar transmission logged years earlier. Like this current transmission, the previous one repeated in a similar pattern. and it was followed in just six months time by an alien crash landing on the Earth's moon.

The confirmation that the prior signal originated from an intelligent alien species that made its way to the Earth's moon is not surprising, given that this particular species has a history that includes Earth.

As part of her high security classification, Sam had access to files, the likes of which rivaled the Vatican Archives. She focused her research on the history of Planet Earth. The files she located and read provided her with a profound look into some aliens species that had been Earth dwellers in ancient times.

## The Trouts

The Trouts are an alien race with incredibly advanced abilities to create and harness energy, travel throughout and between the many universes, heal disease, conceal (camouflage), and destroy. They vary in size and stature, but share two common traits. They are a translucent grey in color and have black, almond shaped eyes.

Present day Trouts are the descendants of an invasive alien race that had previously been fierce conquerers. Before the chain reaction of star explosions (referred to as the Great Destruction) began, the Trouts had managed to conquer a large part of the Andromeda galaxy. Their expansion provided them with the spoils that each new star system had to offer. During their conquests, they had two main objectives. Sourcing energy and seeding planets with their own genome.

Even this most advanced species was not without flaw. They became so powerful that they were able to manipulate energy into creating nebula star systems. This expansive use of their knowledge on harnessing energy came with an unsolvable paradox.

The magnitude of the power they harnessed accelerated at such a fast rate that they were unable to prevent it from getting out of control. The power took on a life of its own that always ended in the star's total self-destruction and the end of any life within that star's planetary system. It was as if power itself concluded that there was no longer any point to existing.

They failed at their attempts to slow the acceleration rate. This meant that they would not be able to end the loop that started with creation and ended with full destruction, leaving nothing but dark energy moving through space. Even worse, while the acceleration rate was increasing, the hosting universe expanded, making it more difficult to contain the energy. Was power demonstrating the concept of learned improvement? What if power could accelerate without external stimulation? If the nature of energy is such that it will inevitably take on a life of its own then slowing the acceleration will only delay, not stop the inevitable.

The Trouts believed they could perhaps break the loop if they could identify the point in time just before the power they created took on a life of its own. The point before the power became conscience of itself and of its ability. The point of no return.

The efforts the Trouts made in their quest to identify the point of no return were unsuccessful. For generations, species after species perished in their home galaxy of Andromeda.

When the Trouts ventured beyond Andromeda to the Milky Way, they intended to try and identify the point of no return by witnessing the natural history progression of evolution in another galaxy. They were interested to find what would happen if they monitored a planet with all its energy evolving at its natural pace. They would not interfere in any way unless if otherwise the planet faced imminent destruction.

The problem they faced was that they were running out of the time they needed to save their own race and the people on Earth needed a jumpstart to advance as a race.

technologically. The Trouts stepped in and provided the information necessary to move evolution along on Earth. Was this an exercise in futility? Once the technology begins to advance, is it already too late to stop the inevitable destruction? Is that the path that leads to the point of no return? Or, is it when a species hands over the reins of control over their future to an uncontrollable energy source?

The Trouts believed that If the point of no return is not identified or if its pointless to try because it has already passed, they could nonetheless use their ability to travel back in time and stop the energy source or slow the process long enough to save a species. This could be why they have been sighted by people on Earth throughout its history. Is there still time to save the human race on Earth from extinction by its own growing energy source?

## The Grendolans

The Grendolans are a reptilian race, agile and quick. By using their ability to camouflage like chameleons, these aliens could blend into almost any background. They also have remarkable adaptability to environmental changes.

On their own planet their species had evolved in such a manner that rendered copulation for fertilization unnecessary. Instead, they relied upon test tube like fertilization. This worked well for several generations.

When this method began to fail, the Grendolans realized that the extinction of their kind was on the horizon, unless they could find a solution to their inability to produce offspring naturally.

While the Trouts mostly stayed away from Earth, preferring to either remain aboard their spacecraft or on the Earth's moon, the Grendolans made themselves at home on Earth without hesitation.

Although they were not always visible, they did make themselves known whenever it suited to advance their curriculum. Unlike the Trouts, the Grendolans preferred to be close to the heart of the Earth. They made use of its underbelly, inhabiting natural caves throughout the western United States. Some believe that it is possible that a line of their descendants still inhabit the underground there and within the walls of the canyons.

## History of the Portals

In ancient times there were portals on Earth. The portals were used as gateways for interstellar transport. The Grendolans used them to travel back and forth between Earth and PCb, their home planet.

Several large portals were later developed as gateways to other planets and orbiting moons in other galaxies. It was through one such portal that the alien species known as the Trouts first came to Earth from their planet in the Andromeda Galaxy.

The Trouts co-existed peacefully with the Grendolans for hundreds of years. They were aligned with the Grendolans in their quest to source and mine the Earth for its raw energy and precious metals. They were also aligned in their intent to advance the intelligence of the human residents on the planet who were predominately living as nomadic tribesmen.

The Trouts and Grendolans were like gods to the early Earth inhabitants and they offered no resistance to their pillage. The aliens needed energy to refuel their spacecrafts and to open and close the portals.

To achieve their harnessing energy goals faster, the Grendolans used the portals to transport giants to Earth. The giants were enslaved to work constructing huge pyramid monuments, many of which remain to present time. These monuments were built by the giants to access the power of the magnetic fields on Earth and the power of its rotating core.

Each pyramid was also designed to include a portal at its highest point. These portals could be used to quickly travel between the pyramids built on every major land mass throughout the Earth. Some portals were built as gateways between earth and its satellite moon.

As is written in the true history, the giants eventually became restless and out of control. There is a legend that tells the tale of a demon sorceress who bewitched the giants, enticing them into committing nefarious acts. There are also accounts that speak of another alien race descending on Earth and battling with the Trouts and Grendolans. Whatever the truth, the giants began to rebel against the aliens.

The Grendolans and Trouts did not agree on the course of action to take with the giants. While the Grendolans wanted to attempt negotiating peace with the giants, the Trouts wanted to destroy them. The Trouts took ownership of the situation and thus the matter into hand. They used a laser weapon to cut down all the large trees on Earth. When the trees were cut, their deep roots released a deluge of water, resulting in the great flooding of the Earth.

At the time of the flood, the Grendolans closed the portals on Earth in order to prevent the giants from escaping the flood.

It was believed that most of the giants perished in the great flood; but, there were reports that some giants survived and retreated underground, escaping into the tunnels that run deep below the iced polar region.

The Trouts returned to their planet during which time a group of Grendolans remained on the Earth's moon until the flood waters receded. Afterward, they established a base within the moon and built a portal there for use as a gateway between the moon and their home planet. They used that portal to return to PCb.

Once back on PCb, the Grendolans returned a drone-like device back to the moon. The drone was purposed to disable the transmitter necessary to operate the moon portal.

For thousands of years, the moon portal and the pyramid portals on Earth remained in a state of disrepair, their existence unknown to mankind.

## Crash Landing

A group of aliens were first captured on earth in 2036 following the crash of their spacecraft in the desert, roughly twenty five miles east of Las Vegas, Nevada. These aliens were Grendolans and their crash on Earth was no accident.

Their commander, a decorated male federation officer, was sent to Earth on a mission to peacefully negotiate the return of Grendolans to Earth. The Grendolans wanted access to the plants on Earth believed to have the medicinal qualities necessary to reverse the cause of the disease that rendered their females sterile. They wanted authorization to send a group of young Grendolans to live on Earth where they would participate in a fertilization vaccine study. Unbeknownst to them, there was already a team on Earth prepared to conduct that study.

The Order had tasked Stoner to negotiate with the Grendolans. They wanted to explore the possibility of using advanced technology to perhaps open or access a wormhole as a means of traveling to another inhabitable planet. Stoner needed a bargaining chip and believed that he found it while reading classified NASA files regarding the pyramids on Earth.

Stoner was cocky enough to outwardly act as though the negotiation was already successful. This tactic, the big bluff, worked beautifully for him because there were so few who were in the “classified inner circle.” At NASA, no one ever called his bluff by requesting that he provide proof of anything. So, when he asked for and obtained access to the Havasupai land for a study by presenting credentials that were totally falsified, no one ever was the wiser.

Stoner was so confident in his chosen A.T.E. that he had already set his plan in motion. He would arrange to host the Grendolans in exchange for their knowledge of advanced technology that would enable him to open a portal.

The commander aboard the crashed spacecraft was loyal to the Federation on PCb. He had no intention of making a crash landing. As it turned out, his intention was not shared by his on-board crew.

The five other crew members worked collectively and mutinied the ship by deliberately sabotaging the craft to crash in the Painted Desert, not far from Tuba City, Arizona. Their plan was to set up residence within a pyramid located within the Grand Canyon, below its north rim.

To assure their crafts's demise, the five did the dirty work necessary by rigging a series of small explosions targeted at the ship's engineering system. It was a daring and dangerous plan. Desperation was their primary motive, if they felt human-like motivation. Otherwise, if they had to justify or defend their actions, they would have likely done so on the premise that they did what was necessary to assure the survival of their kind. Time was of the essence for their generation to establish a fertilization process. They knew that the likelihood of success rested in their ability to begin the process quickly. They also knew that they would need help from humans to bring their plan to fruition. They did not know the price they would pay for the help they required.

The crash landing destroyed their craft's communication system. The explosives that were set off also destroyed all the data records maintained. The memory boards were fried. They counted on this happening. It would be helpful to them and provide them with time to avoid detection by their federation. Once they landed, the alien crew thought they would be free to take up residence on Earth. They didn't consider that their crash landing would render them disabled with injury.

The incoming craft was spotted on radar and tracked to the crash site, where a rescue and recovery team was dispatched. Five of the aliens were picked up discreetly by Stoner and other Air Force personnel. Stoner directed to have them taken to a secret medical facility where efforts would be made to ensure their survival. Once they were stable, the five would be moved to Base 08 L11 where they would remain peacefully for the next two years.

The sixth uninjured alien made its escape during the recovery process. Before the others were taken to the medical facility on Base 08, the sixth Grendolan, the ship's commander, telepathically implanted disinformation to Stoner's crew regarding the number of aliens on the crashed ship. Before Stoner left the crash site, the alien scanned his mind to retrieve information that he quickly found useful.

While Stoner worked on processing the crash site, the alien commander opened a portal and returned to PCb, but not before picking up the insurance policy it learned about while probing Stoner's mind.

Just prior to leaving Earth, the commander sent a detailed message to Stoner's cellphone voicemail. The message was straightforward and was written like a power point presentation. Included within the message were the preliminary talking points of a proposed agreement between the PCb Federation and Earth.

The other aliens were equipped with the same means to open a one-way portal that would transport each of them back to PCb; however, the portable portal pack was automatically disabled if the sensors indicated that its owner was injured, as was the fate of the remaining five. These aliens needed materials to repair their portable portal packs and for the time being, they were at the mercy of Stoner and the Order. They would have to wait for the right opportunity to attempt an escape back to PCb, or better yet, to the Earth's moon base.

If they could take over the moon base, they could convert it into a suitable place to serve as their out post in the Milky Way Galaxy. By doing so, they could have direct and easy access to the native plants believed to possess the cure necessary for their species to copulate successfully.

Access to the plants was just one necessary step in the process. They had been on previous missions and had successfully gathered the plants. But, once transported beyond the Earth's orbit around the Sun the plants lost their potency.

The leader of these five Grendolans was privy to two things upon which they based their plan. First, in order for the medicinal quality of the plants to work, it had to be introduced to the subject as a vaccine while the subject was on Earth. And second, if their mission failed, their species would likely perish at the end of their generation.

# Alien Alliance

Stoner had anticipated that there would be some negotiating between the Order on Earth and the Federation of PCb to acquire the knowledge required for opening the Moon Base Portal and the Earth to Moon portal. He had the authorization by the Order to enter into an agreement with the Grendolans. This authorization came with a great pressure from the Order to assure that an Alliance with the Grendolans was achieved without delay and without the knowledge of the public at large. Stoner had had every intention of realizing a successful outcome; however, the crash landing of the alien's ship changed the plan dramatically.

Now, there would surely be a delay. Now, there was uncertainty. He was not sure that the five aliens would survive for one thing. If they did survive, would they be willing and able to provide the technical knowledge necessary to open the portals thereby advancing Earth's space program and the ability of humans to evacuate the planet? Without operating portals, it is doubtful that the human population will survive on Earth long enough to evacuate to another moon or planet suitable to ensure the continuation of the human species.

One thing was clear. The Earth is nearing the completion of a reset of its north and south poles. For the last twenty years the poles have been shifting at an accelerating rate. The calculated acceleration of the polar shift has revealed that the reset will be complete before the end of the next decade. The ice caps will continue melting and the ocean will rise. All coastal and low lying regions will flood, rending large portions of land under water and uninhabitable.

The affect on the human race will be enormous and catastrophic. Not so for the Grendolans. The Grendolans can live in a water environment and as noted in Earth's historic records, have done so on Earth previously. Stoner thought that returning to Earth in order to claim the planet as their own was their underlying plan. He thought that perhaps the Grendolans believe that if they return to Earth the evolution of their race will revert back to a time when their females were fertile.

It is not certain if the infertility of the Grendolans was caused by disease or some type of virus that spread through their race. The timing of the start of this affliction, having been after they first began experimenting with time travel, was disturbing. Within the passing of only a few generations, the malady is now endemic to their planet. Stoner thought that the PCb Federation believed that if they facilitate a return of their race to Earth, the fertility of their females will also return. How ironic is this, Stoner mused. Here we are about to make an agreement with an alien race to help us leave a planet they want to return to. But with all that has happened, when will any of this be plausible?

While the emergency team in the medical bay worked to keep the five aliens alive, Stoner waited behind the glass partition of the operating room observation deck. He pulled out his cellphone when he heard the ding that told him he had a new email. As he read the message he smiled. All the points of agreement presented by PCb Federation had been anticipated. He had already won. He knew it! He had planned this well and would be praised for this achievement. He read on, then, his smile quickly faded and he turned pale while reading the last sentence of the message.

## The A.T. E. on Base 08

Stoner was in charge of the Grendolans held on Base 08. While secretly held on the base L11, the aliens worked alongside the A.T.E., with the exception of Sam, who remained isolated from the rest. Stoner told Sam and the others that he kept her apart in order that she continue her work analyzing the signals from PCb. In truth, he wanted to minimize the risk of her learning of his hidden agenda.

When most of the other members of the A.T.E. were first introduced to the Grendolans, they were introduced through virtual reality simulation. The earlier lab simulator tests Stoner had ordered were successful in confirming that the results of working in reality mirrored the results while working virtually. Stoner's team merely had to precisely follow the steps they were shown by the Grendolans. In reality, they worked in separate labs; but, virtually, they were side by side. Stoner utilized advanced high tech simulators that were engineered to create avatars for each of them so the Grendolans were unaware of what their human co-workers looked like and vise versa.

Griff was in charge of their team whenever Stoner was absent and he kept everyone on task. He took the lead on scheduling their project checkpoints to assure the completion in accordance with the schedule provided by Stoner.

Griff also developed a portable sound transmitter with the capability of both long range and short burst frequency transmission strong enough to start an avalanche.

This transmitter was a back up for the one already in place at the site of the moon reactor. Activating the existing transmitter was risky because of radiation exposure and the possibility of explosion. Using remotely controlled robots would mitigate this risk. Also, it was unknown if the existing power supply would be too much or too little to operate the existing transmitter. If the power was still flowing and the transmitter was turned on before the oscillator was checked, a surge could result in a fried generator or a non-functioning oscillator and/or modulator.

James and Matthew built the remotely operated robot prototypes. These robots were dexterously capable of the skillful movement required to confirm that the existing power supply was sufficient before roping in the existing transmitter without activating it. The positioning of the transmitter was such that retrieving it required a precise roping skill. Each Matthew and James had acquired the roping skill in their youth and now had the robotic science knowledge needed to program the prototypes.

Once the transmitter is retrieved, they would examine it for functionality, and if working, would set the carrier wave to correspond with the audio signal needed to reopen the moon portal. Lastly, they would send the robots in to replace the transmitter that would now be equipped with a remote activation switch.

While James and Matthew worked with the robots, Finn and Gretchen relied upon their knowledge of behavioral science to monitor them and the other team members for any first hints of stress that could affect their ability to maintain their focus on the tasks at hand. They also kept a daily activities log on the alien avatars, making note of any deviation in their demeanor as the project moved forward.

During this time, Ro worked alone in a L11 lab developing a fertilization vaccine using the plants she and her team were gifted from the Havasupai tribe.

Basque also worked solo in a lab on L11, creating the masks the Grendolans would wear when they are in the presence of humans. Basque was the first one of the A.T.E. to see the Grendolans up close in reality. To his advantage, all of his work in Hollywood had desensitized him to seeing strange looking creatures. He was not at all afraid of them. On the contrary, he was intrigued by their appearance. He quickly learned which of the five was the leader when he saw one of them appearing to instruct the others. That one was also the largest of the males.

Basque completed the masks within a few week, then introduced Ro to the aliens one at a time. She first met the females, both masked. During her initial medical examination, she gently removed their masks. Although there were no spoken words, Ro heard the aliens speaking to her mind and she felt that they were reading her thoughts as she explained each step in the examination process. Ro soon had the samples she needed to further her work on a fertilization vaccine.

Meanwhile, working overnight in her office on L10, Sam had just completed her analysis of the transmissions and immediately called Stoner's cellphone. "What the fuck Sam! It's three o'fucking clock in the morning! What could be so important that could not wait another three hours?" "You are not going to want to wait to hear this sir. I have completed my analysis on that signal we have been concentrating our efforts on and I believe this is what we have been waiting for."

## Escape to the Moon

Nearly three years after their crash to Earth, the five surviving aliens from PCb that were residing on Base 08 in secret transported themselves to the moon. It was believed that they activated a portal on Base 08 to do so. It is also believed that during their stay on Base 08 they were able to repair four of the portable portal packs that were disabled when they crash-landed.

Once on the moon, the five aliens temporarily took charge of the international base established there. They timed their invasion to coincide with the arrival of a civilian pleasure space cruise run by a company funded through Elon Musk. The rogue aliens took six passengers and two crew members hostage. But, the takeover was short-lived. Less than 48 hours later the hostages were released and the aliens were taken into custody.

Several versions of what happened during the siege were posted on the world wide web by main stream news sources and off streamers. The post that went viral, receiving  the most attention and considered the most interesting was the version told that included Musk's civilian influencer passenger.  It was alleged that she was hired to go on the excursion to the moon base free of charge in exchange for a contracted promise to promote the trip on social media. In fact, the influencer was a reporter working under cover for a world wide news network.

It was rumored that this reporter chatted non-stop at the five who held them captive and constantly acted as though she was directing them in her own reality show. She purportedly followed them around while continuously barking instructions and snapping photographs or making video clip recordings. It was said that her actions confused and annoyed the aliens to the extent that they practically surrendered just to get away from her.

It was later discovered that the woman was lucky to have survived the ordeal because she was about to be attacked, but it was unclear if by the aliens or the other civilian passengers, when a special forces team intervened. The masques worn by aliens helped to avoid a more complicated situation.

After the hostages were freed and safely put on an earth-bound flight, the aliens were taken into custody; but, without their portable portal packs. Those were stashed away somewhere on the Receiving Bay.

The captured aliens were escorted to the moon's deepest interior level for holding. This level, referred to as 'The Zoo', was inaccessible without the same security clearance as that on Base 08, L11.

Since the time of their recapture, these turned lately hostiles have been "guests without liberty" within the depths of the hollowed moon.

## The Zoo

The Zoo is a moon base holding pen, for lack of a better description. It was named for the diverse and sometimes exotic captives held within its cage-like enclosures. It's very existence was so controversial that even some world leaders were kept in the dark.

The Zoo captives included humans who were being held for deviant behavior observation. Those offenders in particular were held at the Zoo voluntarily in exchange for various incentives that sometimes included one for an early release from incarceration. The program participants were chosen carefully. They had to pass tests similar to those training astronauts are given. These tests are designed to simulate various conditions they would face on the moon, including being subject to stressful situations. Due to the confidential nature of the project, those chosen were individuals unlikely to have living relatives seeking visitation.

The deviant behavior research program was first introduced on Earth as a crime prevention initiative. It was meant to provide a platform for research of issues related to identifying individuals with deviant behavioral tendencies. If these tendencies could be identified early and prior to the commission of a nefarious act, perhaps there could be intervention methods introduced that may work to prevent future crimes. When word of the program was leaked to the main stream media, exaggerated reports of abuse flooded the internet. After the matter was politicized, Congressional Hearings took place. To avoid a disruption in the program funding, and to silence the media blitz and the politicians, a decision was made by the Order to publicly announce the end of the program.

After the smoke cleared, the Order restarted the research on the moon base. It's present existence there was thought to be the main reason for the reporter going under cover on the civilian pleasure cruise trip to the moon at the time of the Grendolan incident.

The Order received word about the second program leak and prior to the pleasure cruise voyage, decided to move the prisoners in the program to a temporary housing facility on Base 08.

Once the reporter's objective was quashed, the Order gave the green light to restart the program; however, that was put on hold with the capture of the Grendolan aliens who were now occupying the Zoo.

When the Grendolans were recaptured, they were placed inside the only zoo enclosure surrounded by a sound wave barrier generated to block the human brain from receiving or sending telepathic messages.

If irony had a sister, she would be smiling because the Grendolans were the source of the knowledge used to develop the technology that made the barrier system possible.

## Opening the Portals

The team theorized that at the time the portals on Earth were closed, the sound waves required to close them triggered minuscule breaks in the cores of the nuclear reactors that were the source of their power. Since the closure of the portals, the radiation leaks have slowly increased and over time have reached a point where the contamination is believed to have extended out beyond the core.

To compound the issue, recent solar flares from the Earth's sun have become intense and sporadic. This has added another dangerous component to the operations on the moon base. A solar flare hitting the moon would cause a power surge that could interfere with the existing power flow on the moon base. It could also disable surrounding satellites. Scientists studying the sun's activity agreed that a Coronal Mass Ejection would likely occur in the near future and the interaction of the erupted plasma and magnetic field with the Earth's magnetosphere could result in a significant space weather disturbance.

Stoner knew that time was running out to shut down and repair the moon reactor. If left as is and the core melts, the base will likely explode. This happening would be a catastrophic event for planet Earth, likely resulting in the eventual extinction of the human race.

In terms of the pyramids on Earth and their underlying nuclear reactors, they are believed to be stable for the time being. However, if the they each have a portal as is suspected, they too are vulnerable to damage if the portal is haphazardly opened.

The Grendolans had shared their knowledge on how to reopen the portals with the A.T.E. while working with them on Base 08. They needed the humans to provide the materials and hands for building the robots they would need to open the moon portal. Without robots, the process to do so was too dangerous for either them or the humans.

After the Grendolans were recaptured, Stoner deployed the A.T.E. to the moon to resume their work. Finn and Gretchen were tasked with studying the aliens in captivity, keeping case notes regarding their interactions. They would make special note of any behavioral changes.

Ro ran the medical bay with Basque as her assistant. They kept incident and weekly summary logs on each of the A.T.E. and the five aliens.

Matthew and James tested the robots Stoner had transported to their lab, situated next to the Reactor Bay. Their knowledge of robotics and roping skills provided the tools they needed to move forward with testing their programming.

Griff, with an assist from an old colleague, installed a temporary power grid for their use to test the transmitter when retrieved. To avoid exposure to any residual radiation near the cooling tower, they donned protective suits while installing a layer of lead surrounding the concrete shield in place around the reactor's tower. This additional layer of protection was deemed prudent by Stoner and the team agreed. Stoner's order that this safety precaution remain in place after the nuclear reactor reboot provided the team with some reassurance that he had their back.

Stoner also gave the order that the robots and not any of their team would retrieve the existing transmitter. Once the transmitter was safely disconnected from the reactor, Griff and his team could shut down the reactor from a distance, then send the robots in to make any necessary repairs.

Once the reactor is repaired, the A.T. E. will initiate a reboot with the help of the maintenance team stationed on the moon. As a precaution against any lingering radiation exposure, the robots would reinstall the portal transmitter.

According to the plan, the A.T.E. would test the transmitter with the sequence of sound waves they were given by the Grendolans to confirm the reopening of the portal. What was planned to happen at this point varies, depending on who's viewpoint was considered.

The majority of team A.T.E. believed that they would safely neutralize the moon reactor, have it repaired and restarted before reopening the portal. Opening a portal would instantly expand Earth's space exploration program and make it possible to evacuate at least some of the human race, thus avoiding extinction in the event of an imminent catastrophic event.

Ro and Basque thought that once the portal was operational they would welcome the first transport of young Grendolan females to the moon base, where they would be quarantined before their transport to Earth.

After clearing them earthbound, the couple would return to their waiting medical team on Base 08. There, they would continue the vaccination program they had secretly started.

Ro's fertilization research, and her newly gained insight regarding the Grendolan's gestation period, led her to conclude that the vaccine she developed has a good chance of success. Even if this project remained secret to everyone but her small team, she didn't care. It was enough to know she had done something to play a part in saving a race from extinction.

The Grendolans planned that one of them would return to PCb then begin to transport subjects from PCb to the moon base. If they controlled the moon, they would also be in a position to control a portal there. This portal would be used exclusively to travel between Earth and its moon.

On Earth they would access the plants needed to make a fertilization vaccine. Working alongside Ro had given them the knowledge they needed to make the vaccine. Their females would be transported from PCb to Earth where they would receive the vaccine treatment in the pyramid situated near the North Rim of the Grand Canyon. Once inoculated and confirmed to be carrying an offspring, the female Grendolan would open a portable portal on that pyramid to return to PCb.

The five Grendolans knew that their federation on PCb, to which they had at one time pledged their allegiance, would have questioned the absence of their crew commander's communication. Because they were injured at the time of the crash landing, they were unaware that their commander had escaped death and capture and had returned to PCb.

Although they believed their commander had died in the crash, they also believed that their federation would send probes. They likely had already sent a tracker and had knowledge of their time on Base 08. They are on borrowed time to prove that their plan was the right one, the best one to follow. They would save their species and advance the human race at the same time. What they did to get to this point, including sacrificing their commander, was necessary, and, if they cared at all about justification, that would have been sufficient. But instead, they are now within the bowels of the Earth's moon awaiting their fate.

Nearly four years ago they thought that they had chosen the right person when striking a deal with Stoner to reopen the Earth and moon portals. Stoner had the authority they needed to put the next phase of their plan in motion. That plan was flawed. The aliens had probed Stoner's mind and discovered that he intended to double-cross them. That made it necessary to activate the Base 08 portal early and execute their coup on the moon.

It was true that Stoner intended to deceive the Grendolans, but he needed them to believe that they had good odds of taking over the moon base. He also wanted them to activate the Base 08 portal, so he had undergone a treatment that altered his memory to include false information. When they probed his mind they learned (or so thought) that the security forces on the moon were temporarily reduced leaving only a skeleton crew in charge.

Stoner knew that because the transmission from PCb signaled the eminent return of the Grendolan Federation, it was time to secure the renegades and prepare for the Federation's arrival. He intended to have the moon portal open as planned. The underlying Order mission, to have at least one evacuation from Earth route operational, would be accomplished with the opening of the portal. His plan would work.

After the Grendolan's failed coup attempt, Stoner decided to hold them as a good will chip to show his alliance with the PCb Federation. He was smug about what he felt sure was a smart move. He intended to hand them over to the PCb Federation representatives upon their arrival. Returning his captures to the Grendolan Federation was not just a gesture of good will. For Stoner, it was the guarantee of a successful hostage exchange. If his team could do something to save the Grendolan race in the process, well that was just a bonus.

## Base 08 Portal

“Gear up and meet me in the L11 tunnel at the carts in one hour.” Damn! He knows that I’ve been in the tunnel! I don’t even know why that would surprise me. Fucking Stoner has eyes everywhere. Sam grimaced as she pulled her flight gear out of the locker inside her bedroom closet. Less than five minutes later she was back in the tunnel below L11.

“What now?” she asked when Stoner appeared out of an elevator she had not previously known existed. He shot her a hard look and said “get in” as he turned back toward the elevator opening. He waited until the door was fully closed before touching a button on the keypad that was engineered to work only at the touch of someone who had a live finger with the pre-programed fingerprint. Sam remembered reading about the technology used for such security. The newer improved version avoided the useless maiming of a person to acquire a finger. There was still risk of personal harm to the print-bearer; but, because the locks were well hidden and sparingly used, potential damages were lessened.

The elevator ascended at a moderate rate of speed for about ten seconds before it came to a gentle stop. When the door opened, Sam saw the +7 written on the inside elevator wall plaque. Stoner picked up his gear from the floor then quickly moved forward. Once out of the elevator, he gestured toward a closed door. “After you Sam.“ Sam turned the door handle and stepped onto the same small stair landing she had ended up on after having spent her lunch break exploring the tunnels and trudging up flights of stairs. The same landing with a door she could not open.

She swung back around just in time to see that the door they just passed through appeared to melt into the wall as it closed. She gave Stoner a puzzled look, then followed his pointing finger directing her attention to the other door.

"Open it Sam." "I can't. I tried when…" "Yeah I know, when you were here the first time. What you didn't try then will work now. Use the amulet on your necklace." Sam carefully removed her necklace then placed the amulet into the infinity shaped impression in the keypad on the wall next to the door.

The door slid open, revealing a small, closet sized, triangular-shaped room. Once Sam and Stoner stepped inside and onto the grated platform floor, the door slid shut behind them.

"What is this place?" Sam asked as she took a quick look around. "This is a portal Sam. It has been here for centuries. I'll explain more later, but right now we need to use it before it's too late."

"Where does it lead?" asked Sam, her voice starting to rise. "It should open within the receiving bay level on the dark side of the moon. That's where the escaping aliens were first caught on security cameras, so that's where I believe it will open."

"Where you believe the escaping aliens were first seen? What escaping aliens? Are you fucking kidding me right now? Why would I trust what you believe? You know what I believe Stoner? I believe you are fucking crazy! You are crazy and you are sadly mistaken if you think I'm going to follow you into never never land because you believe something. Aliens Stoner? Really? When were you going to fill me in about that? No, no, no Stoner! I'm staying right here until you ..."

Before Sam could finish, Stoner pushed a button on his wristwatch. The tiny room began to vibrate and they were surrounded by a faint humming sound that grew slowly grew louder. The wall in front of them transformed from solid to translucent and the grated floor beneath their feet began to vibrate.

"What's going on here Stoner? You fucker! You are not doing this! I..." Sam cried with disbelief. Suddenly the portal that was open before them grew large enough to walk through. At that instant, Stoner grabbed Sam by the arm pulling her with him through to the other side.

## Testing the Robots

For the past three hours Mathew and James have been testing the two robots they built with the help of the now incarcerated five aliens. They have been running variations of a drill, with a focus on tossing ropes.

One rope is looped with an attached snare designed to latch around a pin that secures the receiver to the protruding wall plate attached to the affixed ladder on the inside of the cooling tower. A second rope is looped like a rope would be when used to lasso a steer during a rodeo, except much smaller in scale. This second rope will be tossed around the receiver.

Once in place, the snare on the first rope closes taught around the pin. The robots are programmed to pull out the pin and at the same time pull up on the rope that secures the receiver. The precise timing of the rope handling is critical to the success of retrieving the receiver from the cooling tower without any further damage to it or damage to the reactor.

The team decided that taking this course of action is the only way to retrieve the receiver safely, without the need for biological exposure to the reactor's leaking radiation.

The process of recovery was not without some risk. If the receiver is damaged because it comes into contact with the cooling tower wall while being raised, or worse, if it is dropped, the portal opening would likely be delayed.

Stoner did not consider that outcome a possibility, and therefore never brought up a fail scenario when discussing the recovery process with the A.T.E. This mission would succeed as planned. It had to succeed. That was Stoner's only option.

Once the receiver is retrieved, both robots will descend into the cooling tower, assess damage to the reactor, and make any necessary repair. The team, led by Griff, will monitor and instruct throughout the assessment and repair.

The good news the team had was that the radiation level detected at the top of the cooling tower was relatively low. The team was hopeful that the radiation leakage previously detected was merely the residual affect of closing the portal and not due to a leaking reactor.

Some of the team also theorized that the portal was not completely closed to gamma and X-rays but they were unable to test this because they were unable to confirm the exact portal location. It should be in the rear of the Receiving Bay because that is the largest area of free space. That would make the most sense: but, what makes sense to them now may be irrelevant. Even when using sensitive equipment designed to identify the presence of radiation, the results were inconclusive. Regardless, a newly installed receiver will solve that dilemma as long as the transmitter functioned the way it should.

So far, the robots are performing well. Matthew and James named the robots C1 and C2 (short for Cibers 1 and 2, though their inside joke was that their real names were Cowboys 1 and 2.

"Now Matt, I'm going to move on to phase II, the bots lowering rope down a hole and descending the tower to test the depth perception and target recognition programming."

Each robot was pre- programed to perform every task: but, their movements could be altered in motion if need be. They were interchangeable and that reduced the overall risk of project failure. They were programmed to recognize when they descended to a depth that was calculated to be at a point exactly opposite to the location of the receiver. This was a failsafe precaution since both robots had full sight sensory capabilities.

"Look who's joining the party," Matthew said as Griff walked in the room. "Hey, or should I say houdy to my favorite bot programmers? Looks like you've been busy, and I'm guessing that Stoner hasn't seen the the hats?" Griff gestured to the robots that were standing to the side of the monitoring station. Each was wearing a Stetson cowboy hat and C1 had a painted on mustache. "Affirmative on that; but, in our defense, it helped the visual aspect of our programming," explained James.

"It won't even raise an eyebrow if the plan succeeds," Griff responds. "Stoner isn't that stuffy, at least not all the time. I agree that he's been more on edge than usual, but considering the alien episode, who can blame him?"

"Let's go over the plan," suggests Matthew. "Sure," James said as he picked up a tablet from the monitor desk. "Matt and I will remote the bots. C1 will carry a radiation monitor down into the tower and place it on the wall near the receiver. Griff, you will monitor the readings from this position. Once the monitor is in place, C1 will throw the first rope." "Yes, to secure a hold on the receiver," continues Mathew. "Then, once C2 descends the tower, C1 tosses the other end of the rope to C2. C2 ascends the tower holding the rope, letting out slack as needed. When C2 has reached the top of the tower, C1 throws a second rope around the pin that holds the receiver to the wall bracket. The tricky part comes next. C1 has to pull the pin with one hand while C2 holds the receiver as steady as possible with the other. We don't want to find out what happens if the receiver is knocked into the reactor. When the pin is pulled and the receiver is free, C2 hoists the receiver up to the top." "Easy peasy for bots, hey?"

"Let's hope so. Don't want to disappoint the big bug," James said as he made a few entries on his tablet. "Once the old receiver is retrieved, we can safely begin the reactor reboot cycle. While it's shutdown, we can sweep the tower for cracks in the casing and make any necessary repairs."

Matthew takes over. "The bots will secure the new receiver that the team developed with the aliens. With that in place, we can restart the reactor, send the transmission and hopefully synchronize the opening of the portal in the Receiving Bay with the arrival of the PCb Federation." Griff nods his approval.

"Stoner wants to be on deck for the bot performance test so text me when you're ready. I'll be with Gretchen and Finn in the their lab reviewing the latest readings on recent signals from PCb that they are analyzing. We are getting closer to go time for the Federation's arrival." That said, Griff left the Texans to their cowboy robots.

## Medical Emergency in the Zoo

Ro and Basque were working in a separate lab when the alarm sounded. A calm, disinterested voice spoke over the intercom system summoning Doctor Ro O'Leary. It seemed that there was an incident in progress and her presence was requested immediately. She was to proceed directly to the Holding Bay.

Ro looked at Basque and said, "Right on time. A full moon and now this." "My wife is superstitious? Who knew?" Ro returned Basque's big smile. The truth was, they both knew immediately that this meant that there was trouble in the Zoo.

When Ro saw that Basque moved to join her she hesitated. "Do you think you should come with?" "Not a chance that I'm gonna let you go in there solo," was his reply. "Okay, let's go," Ro said, picking up her medical bag as she turned toward the door. The couple exchanged glances then made their way out the lab door and down the round corridor toward the Holding Bay where the five aliens were detained.

Ro slid her security badge through the transponder slot to unlock the heavy door. The Zoo, officially called the Holding Bay, took up roughly two-thirds of the moon's sub level four, leaving the remainder for several work stations, a small kitchen and break room, a few unisex restrooms, and a control room. They headed toward the control room.

There was no mistaking the purpose of the equipment inside the Holding Pen Control Room. This was a high tech monitoring surveillance system set up. It reminded Basque of a set he once visited in the Los Angeles, California area.

The film set was constructed to appear like a 911 call command center, where all the workers sat at stations in a room kept deliberately dark. The only light sources originated from the system map monitors overhead, the low light desk lamps, and the ceiling lights in the outside corridor that released harsh luminescent light that flooded in whenever someone opened the door.

The work stations with the goose necked lamps and computer monitors were situated at intervals along a room length counter below a grouping of flat screens that were mounted high on the wall. The screens that were turned on appeared to be live-streaming the pen where the five aliens were held. Each screen showed a different angle view of the pen. Two young men at the station turned their attention to Ro and Basque and stood up upon their approach.

"Dr. O'Leary, we haven't had the pleasure. I'm Jake and this is Steuben." "Captain Steuben Smith ma'am and this is Captain Jake Grin, who it seems has forgotten the proper way to make an introduction." "No worries Captain. It's refreshing to have a bit of informality around here." Ro smiled at Jake as she extended her hand to Steuben. "Please call me Ro. This is my husband and lab partner Basque," Ro said as he took a step forward to shake their hands.

Ro moved toward Jake's work station and saw a video game playing on his screen. Jake witnessed this and quickly moved passed her to switch off the monitor screen. Ro looked away pretending she hadn't seen anything. "We were summoned to report here?" Ro gave Basque a "you take over look" then stepped back. Basque took a step toward the counter and pointed up at the overhead screens. "So, what's going on Captains?"

"I'll roll back this morning's footage to 08:00 and replay it on the far right screen so you can see for yourselves. Have a seat."Jake gestured toward a couple of chairs. Ro and Basque settled into two of the lounging chairs behind the work station and waited. "This won't take long," Jake continued. As he walked away Ro overheard Steuben say to Jake, "I'll take the first lunch at 12:00."

When the far right screen came alive the reel showed a straight forward view of the pen with the five aliens standing together in the middle of the enclosure. "Looks like they're in a huddle. Have you seen them do that?" Ro turned to Basque. "Only every time I completed a new masque. When it was first put on. It was like they were collectively agreeing to it." "Or accepting it?" suggested Ro.

Suddenly two of the aliens fell to the floor. "What just happened? Did we miss something?" Basque looked at Ro. The reel continued to the end with the three standing aliens lifting the two fallen onto cots in the pen. Ro shook her head slowly then said, "It looks like they fainted. I need to have access immediately." Ro stood up. "Contact Stoner to clear my access Captains. My partner and I will wait in the Holding Pen."

Anyone who experienced the Holding Bay in person understood why it was referred to as the Zoo. Each pen within was labeled with the name of the species held inside. In some cases, the label Identified the inhabitant(s) merely by a pre-disposed characterization.

As they walked past a few of the empty pens, Ro could not help but read the labeled signs fastened to the outside, still describing the past inhabitants. She got a chill at seeing the signs. “This is just like a zoo Basque. So disturbing to imagine how the prisoners felt in one of these.” “I don’t think their feelings were of any consideration hon. Living in one of these is torture in and of itself.” They reached the far side of one of the larger pens that was void of inhabitants but still furnished. The pair slowly made their way around to the side wall of the pen where they could see right through to the adjacent one.

The pen was divided into two sections by a thick glass or maybe plexiglass partition. The right half looked like a children’s daycare center. There was a sitting area next to a fully stacked bookshelf, several play stations filled with toys, each partitioned off with stackable Lego-like blocks. In the center sat an arts and crafts table that held the remains of an unfinished project. Several sheets of colored paper had been cut into various shapes, some of which had been affixed along the edges of a picture frame and held in place with a glue stick that sat, lid off, on the table.

The left section was sparsely furnished, like that of a jail cell. There was a table, a lamp, a chair, a cot-like bed, and a filled bookshelf.

As they slowly walked past, Ro softly mumbled to Basque, “I wonder whether Finn or Gretchen have heard about this place.” “Even if they have, I doubt that either would ever agree to be involved with this type of social experiment,” Basque replied. “What type of person would come up with this?” Ro continued as the pair made their way further into the holding area. “The type of sick fuck that belongs in one of these…cages for sure. But then, that reasoning places me just about on the same sub level as that of whoever designed this place, right?" "I'm with you on that Basque. It's sick; but I have heard that there was a volunteer program. An alternative to incarceration option available in some extreme cases. . . like when rehabilitation efforts failed. Still, I agree that this is twisted."

Basque stopped suddenly when they reached the front and he saw the plaque describing the former inhabitant above the entry. "Holy shit!" was all he said. It was enough to get Ro's attention. She stared up in disbelief, slapping her hand over her mouth. The sound of her reply was muted by the sudden sharp sound of metal grating on metal. The couple turned their attention to the front of the alien pen situated about 15 yards ahead. They saw that the three standing aliens had lifted a cot from the floor and were attempting to wedge it into the pen at such an angle as to block its entrance.

When they were a little closer to the pen holding the five aliens they could see that in the far left rear of the pen two of the five were lying on cots. "Looks like those two females are in the same position as they were in at the end of the rolled back footage we just viewed. Their eyes appear open though. They look conscience to me. What do you think Ro?" "Hmmm, yes they both look conscience from this distance."

The female Grendolans were slightly smaller in stature than their male counterparts. They also had similar body curves as that of a human woman except those were much less pronounced. Their eyes were a bit larger and rounder and this made them appear more open than those of the males that had slanted, narrower eyes.

Ro and Basque discovered that there were females among the five captives when she and Basque had initially analyzed the fluid samples they had taken. She shared the information with Stoner, who said that having females of the Grendolan species in captivity could provide good leverage if needed in the negotiation process. He instructed Ro to keep the information quiet.

It was easy for Ro to obey Stoner's commands as far as the others were concerned; but, Ro never followed such instruction where Basque was concerned. She decided that if Stoner expected her to withhold information from her husband, he was sadly mistaken.

Ro and Basque were aligned in their partnership and had no intention of forwarding Stoner's political agenda, especially when they had gained the trust of the aliens they had worked with over these past few years.

The next sound was they heard was Captain Grin who had entered the bay, informing them that Ro and only Ro had clearance to enter the pen.

"That may be a bit more difficult now," Basque said as he pointed to the pen gate, now blocked with a cot. Ro looked at the pen then back to the two men. "You can leave now. I've got this." Though hesitant at first, both agreed after Ro assured them that she would not, under any circumstance, take any unnecessary risk.

When the aliens observed Basque and Captain Grin exit the floor, the males removed the cot barricade and stood aside. The females, seeing Ro approaching with her medical bag, immediately sat up on their cots. Ro gestured a stay seated motion to them, then made her way to the pen gate.

She punched a code into the keypad and stepped inside when the gate opened. Once inside, the gate swung shut as Ro walked over to the females still sitting on the cots. Twenty minutes later, Ro left the pen.

When Basque saw her smile greeting him in the outer bay corridor, he knew at once what it meant. He smiled back at her before confirming. "So we keep the celebration of our success quiet and wait for the right timing to act." "You betcha," answered Ro as she grabbed his hand and gave it a squeeze.

While walking back to their lab they discussed the risks of the alliance they made. They would help and protect these aliens, even at the risk of their professional reputation. All things considered, that may be the least of all the risks they faced.

Once back in the outer corridor, Ro handed Basque a computer stick and a small remote. She started to fill Basque in on her plan when she was interrupted by the sound of his cellphone announcing receipt of a new text.

Basque read the text, then showed it to Ro."Looks like it's go time. Didn't you get the text? Your phone's not off is it?" "No, it's not off. Let's head over to the cooling tower observation for the bot performance test, but; it's time for lunch. We need to make a stop back to the control room first."

## Signals from PCb

Finn stood up from his ergonomic work chair to stretch. "This last group of signals you found definitely has my attention Gretchen." "At least something feels right about this assignment. Sometimes I forget that we are social scientists Finn. It feels like we were put on this project because Stoner needed two high clearance analysts that can keep their mouth shut. But, aside from that, I'm glad that at least we're making progress on the scans."
"Yup. Stoner will be happy to hear that the signal interval increase is on track with the time projections for the Federation's arrival and pass through the portal."

Griff walked in and went straight to the printer that was spitting out the latest reading from the scanned area of deep space and PCb. "So this is why Stoner pressed the accelerator?"

"Affirmative," answered Finn. "Gretchen and I have confirmed the readings that Sam had analyzed and we are in total agreement, but don't tell her that Stoner had us working on the same assignment here that she has on Base 08." "No worries there," replied Griff.

"Why does he favor her so much anyway?" Gretchen asked. "They seem to have a strange relationship. She is supposedly a lower ranking officer yet gets a cushy assignment below while we are slaving up here. If it turns out that they are romantically involved I may get sick. He's old enough to be her father and then some."

"No, they don't have that type of relationship. His coddling may stem from his feelings of guilt over the death of her mother. They worked together and word is that he didn't attend her funeral," added Griff.

"Stoner has feelings? A person with feelings would have been there at the funeral showing the family support. I haven't ever seen Stoner show feelings," Finn stated.

"Seriously though, there's more to their story. I just know it," Gretchen asserted. "Okay, okay, enough of the social analysis of Stoner's human behavior Gretchen," answered Griff. "Okay, but; you know the jury's still out on whether or not Stoner is human," Gretchen said with a sly smile as she turned back to her computer.

Griff pulled Finn aside. "So what's with her?" "I guess she feels a bit hood winked by Stoner. Sitting behind a computer analyzing these signals ain't exactly a social scientist's dream job." "Yeah, I get it. Well it's about to get real interesting. Mathew and James reported a go with the bot test. They are about to complete the performance test and replace the receiver. If all goes well we can signal test the transmitter. So let's go."

## The Receiving Bay

Stoner and Sam exited the portal to find themselves on the moon's Receiving Bay. This bay was located directly three levels above the Zoo and one level below the surface of the moon's dark side.

"The team will be joining us later. Before they get here, I need to fill you in on a few things Sam. Most importantly, you must understand that I had good reason to keep you in the dark up to this point. You have to believe me when I tell you that you have always been one of the most important persons in my life and that I would never have done anything to deliberately harm you."

Stoner talking like that was either a joke or the prelude to receiving some nasty work assignment. The last time he alluded to his not wanting to put me in harms way was when he registered me into the flight training program without my knowledge. Yeah, that was just great, waking up to find I was scheduled to be in an anti-gravity chamber the majority of the day. And today? He basically pulled me through an untested portal! What is Stoner up to now? Just as her mind began racing with these thoughts, they suddenly stopped at the sight of Steve approaching from the far side of the bay.

Sam swung around to Stoner, and with a half-angry look on her face said, "What the fuck is this Stoner?" "Take it easy Sam. Steve came here to test our equipment and join the team testing the robots that were built on Base 08. He has been instrumental in identifying and making the necessary adjustments to rectify a few system flaws with our transmitter here. Aside from that, what I have to say to you involves Steve too. Now, let's the three of us find a quiet room to sit down and have a civil private chat."

Sam threw up her arms in disbelief. "Is he why you brought me here Stoner. Is this your idea of couples therapy?" Steve put both hand forward. "Hey Sam, I'm just as shocked as you are about all this and just like you, I have been kept in the dark by this asshole."

"All right! Take it easy and watch yourself Steve. I may not be your regular commander, but on this moon base, I'm in charge. I am trying to talk straight to the two of you now so let's . . . ." Stoner was cut off by an incoming text to his cellphone.

After reading the text he looks up at the angry pair. "They're ready to complete the bot test and if all goes well, replace the receiver. With that accomplished we can initiate the process to open the base portal." Stoner took a quick look between Sam and Steve then said over his shoulder as he was leaving the bay, "Text Ro and Basque. Tell them to meet us in the cooling tower observation room. We'll finish our meeting later."

Sam released a heavy sigh as she watched Stoner exit. She sent the text then turned to Steve and said, "Can you believe him? I swear, if you had seen what he did to get me here. . . "

"It's good to see you Sam." Hearing Steve's deep soft voice had an unexpected affect on Sam. All the years of existing in a world where being tough and holding her own just to get by and retain her sanity quickly faded. His presence brought her back into her previous world, where it was him and her, together, in the type of love that lasts a lifetime. It was the first time Sam felt this way since Maddie's disappearance.

She needed to sit down and before she knew what was happening Steve put an arm around her and led her to a seating area. "Sam, I've been thinking about why Stoner sent for me and I don't think it was just because I am good at diagnostics. There are plenty of others here who could have done what I have. I don't want to upset you Sam, but I think it has something to do with Maddie. I think Stoner has information about her. What doesn't make sense to me is why now? Why did he wait until now to send for me? Is there any reason you are aware of?"

"I have known Stoner all of my life Steve and I still can't figure him out. If I open an Internet browser then type in the phrase "illusive son of a bitch," I would not be surprised if the search result shows a picture of Stoner."

Steve continued. "When I received the opportunity to work at Marshall I figured it was just good luck after all we had been through. It seemed like a good chance for us to have the space that we both needed. Now, as I think back on it, I think that it was all a bit too convenient. I think Stoner manipulated my move so that he could manipulate your move to Base 08. Again, I can't figure out why. From what Griff has told me, the ability to analyze deep space transmissions isn't exactly rare talent around Base 08. Don't get me wrong, you are the very best at what you do, but why did he keep you there in isolation while he had the rest of the team working together?"

Sam sat up closer to the edge of their shared sofa. "I agree that Stoner is manipulative. I'm not defending him but that is his job, to get his team to do what he wants while only sharing as little information as possible. As pissed off as I have been because of the way he has handled some things, I have to admit that I have always felt safe around him."

Sam rose to her feet. "I will ask him straight out to tell us what he is hiding if he doesn't come clean with us. I promise you that." She reached over as Steve rose from the sofa and put her hand in his then said,"It is good to see you too Steve, I have missed us." Steve smiled at her then gave her hand a squeeze."We are in this together Sam. Let's go."

## Sabatage

Ro and Basque entered the Holding Bay Control Room just in time for first lunch. Steuben was leaving on break and Jake was occupied at the back of the room with an in progress information dump print.

Jake glanced up and said, “you back already?” Ro quickly went over to his work station and could see the same video game playing on his computer screen. Jake sprinted across the room and quickly turned off his computer screen. “I, uh, was just. . .” “No need,” Ro said as she put both hands up. “Can you confirm that the sound wave thoughts scrambler is working properly?”

The young man got up and immediately went to a keyboard situated on the console of a work station located at the far right side of the room. While Jake was busy waking up the monitor screen, Basque casually placed a stick into a slot of the hard drive on Steuben’s work station. Just as he expected, Steuben hadn’t shut down his computer when he left for lunch.

The automatic upload would be completed in roughly 15 seconds. In her peripheral vision, Ro could see Basque standing close to Steuben’s station. She needed to keep Jake distracted a little while longer.

After the overhead screen came to life, Ro watched the continuous waves moving across its center. It looked like a vitals monitor common in a medical setting, except that there were no wave spikes and the sound was of a frequency not audible by the human ear.

"There it is ma'am. Is there anything else I can do for you?" "Yes Jake. You can explain why the monitor screen was asleep when we came in." "That's because it could burn out pretty fast if we left it on. We know it's working because, well, I can't share that information without authorization ma'am; but, rest assured it's working."

"That's good Jake because I have to go back into the holding pen. I left my phone there. I just needed to be sure the scrambler is working before I go back in. Oh, and I would appreciate your discretion on this Jake. Stoner would have my head if he found out." "No worries there ma'am." Then Jake gestured to his computer and asked, "Can I trust that my discretion will be reciprocated?" Ro nodded a yes and gave Jake a quick wink.

When the young man leaned forward to switch off the monitor and his back was still turned, Basque removed the stick and then activated the hand-held device he had in his pocket to check if he could activate the program he had uploaded. He watched as the quick blink of light on the overhead monitor confirmed that the program he upload was running before he switched it off.

"That went well," Basque filled a tense silence as the couple made their way along the outer corridor. "As long as those officers monitoring the holding pen don't discover that we sabotaged the brain wave blocker and we can activate a hologram in the aliens's pen, we are golden."

"I'm getting stressed Basque." Ro shook her head then turned to her partner. "Are you sure that we're not forgetting something?" "We followed your plan to the letter Ro. We are about to reap the fruit of years of labor. You just need to relax. What could we have possibly forgot?" "I don't know, I just have this feeling that we forgot something important. Wait! I know! Give me your phone." With that said, Ro sent a text. She looked over at Basque and said, "Now we need to go back to the holding pen to get my phone."

Ro explained. "I sent an instructional text to my phone for the aliens to plant the hologram image into Jake and Steuben's minds when I leave the pen with my phone. I also gave them the passcode they need to open the gate to their pen. Right about now the aliens should be reading it." Ro handed back Basque's phone. "Once I have my phone and we leave the Zoo, you can shut down the brain wave barrier. We'll know if the plan works soon enough. Either the aliens escape undetected or they trip an alarm that could land all of us in a pen." Ro showed Basque her crossed fingers.

## Hologram

Ro unlocked the door to the Holding Bay and strolled right over to the pen holding the five aliens. She resisted looking up toward the cameras. Captain Grin will be expecting to see her there. She would just need to be careful not to stay there too long.

If Stoner suddenly appears, she would say that she had mistakenly left her phone and was just retrieving it. That was actually the truth, well, the last part anyway. When she reached the alien's pen she opened the gate with her access card and walked in.

In the control room, Jake sat at his console waiting for Steuben to return from his lunch break. He glanced up to see Ro enter the alien pen, then turned his attention back to the video game still playing on his computer monitor.

Ro exited the pen and quickly left the Holding Bay. Basque flipped the switch on the device in his pocket as soon as he saw her walk through the door and into the outer corridor. The monitors in the control room blinked once undetected then showed nothing unusual in the Holding Bay. No alarm went off, no disruption appeared in the running security footage. Everything appeared status quo.

Ro and Basque knew that Jake would take his lunch break when Steuben returned and that would provide an additional half hour's time. Time needed to execute the next phase of their alien alliance plan.

With the sound barrier down, one of the five aliens maintained a mind probe projecting the hologram on Jake while the others left the pen.

The four aliens headed for the Receiving Bay where they had stashed away the portable portal packs they used to get from Base 08 to the moon.

Ro and Basque made their way to the Cooling Tower Control Room.

## Robotic Success

Stoner walks into the Cooling Tower Control Room of the Reactor Bay and finds that Gretchen and Finn are already sitting in observation chairs.

Stoner switched on the intercom. "Matthew and James, confirm you are ready to retrieve and replace the receiver." After a brief pause he continues. "Do we have confirmation gentlemen?"

James and Mathew, dressed in hazmat type radiation suits, come into view with the two robots following closely behind.

Ro and Basque entered the room and take a seat just before hearing James's muted voice from inside his helmet. "All is a go start sir. Repairs are complete. The bots are prepped and we ran through two trials on the transmitter replacement program without error."

"Then what are you waiting for? I'm growing old waiting here," Stoner said impatiently. James resisted a short quip back at Stoner, deciding instead to give a look to James understood between them-What an asshole!

Twenty minutes later the robots ascended from the cooling tower with the old receiver and a radiation detector firmly in tow. Matthew took the receiver to Griff waiting in the isolation booth, while James gave a thumbs up to Stoner and the others in the control room.

James had been monitoring the radiation readings throughout the test and by the gesture made told the others the results were good.

"Let's move it forward team. The PCb Federation are on the way and I don't need to repeat myself by telling you the importance of completing this phase of the mission timely.

This time it was Finn and Gretchen sharing a look. Gretchen leaned over to Finn and whispered,"This phase? As if he's shared anything to inform us about the next phase."

"Get that new receiver in place." When Stoner said this he could see that the robots already had the new receiver and were heading back down the ladder. But that was Stoner, always barking orders even if they were redundant.

Stoner goes on,"Griff, is the transmitter ready?" "Affirmative sir. All ready to fire up as soon as the new receiver is in place. Standing by." Stoner clapped and said, "First good news of the day. Stay alert people. You are about to witness an extraordinary moment in history."

The door opens with Sam and Steve walking in hand in hand. Stoner gives them a quick glance then gestures toward the seating area. Ro and Gretchen wave a hello their way while Finn and Basque give them a rhumbs up.

Ten minutes later, James reported the completion of the transmitter replacement. Griff drew in a deep breath then started the sound transmitter.

The silent hush that had swept the room was suddenly interrupted by the shrill sound of an alarm indicating a breach at the  Zoo.

## Code Black

Stoner put up his hand and shouted, "Nobody leaves this room until I say!"

He pushes the intercom button and continues, "Code Black! Griff, shut down the transmitter. James and Mathew, secure the robots and stay with them until you hear from me. Secure this bay after we leave. Sam and Steve, stay here and try to get a live feed on the escapees. Griff, Basque, Finn and Gretchen, pair up and spread out. Search this level. Everyone set your stun guns on disable. I want the aliens recaptured alive and unharmed. Don't take any chances. Text me if you locate them. The base security will contain all the other levels. Ro, you're with me. We're going to the Zoo. Stay alert everyone. This could get ugly."

As he stood up to leave, Basque grabbed Ro and gave her a quick hug. "Be careful hon. See you once we get them back in our pocket."

## Four Aliens Escape

As the others scattered in different directions, Stoner looked at Ro."Maybe on the way to the Zoo's Control Room you can fill me in on what happened when you were called there on a medical emergency earlier today."

Ro resorted to standard procedure and said,"I'm sure you'll want to start by viewing the same footage I did when I was called there this morning."

When they get to the control room, Ro could see that the sound barrier screen was on but there were no waves moving across.

She reached into her pocket to find that Basque had slipped in the remote device. She pressed the kill switch that blocked the sound wave barrier program Basque had installed earlier.

The sound barrier screen came to life with a constant series of waves moving across it's center. Captains Jake and Steuben both jolted as though they had just received a mild electrical shock.

The security camera live footage continued to roll as usual. At first it seemed like perhaps the incident was just caused by a system malfunction. All of the pen security cameras were live streaming the pens as captured on a multi view screen with a view of all twelve pens. It was hard to see any detail because the size of each pen was so small.

The Captains were busily checking the function of all the pen cameras when Stoner said,"Pull up the alien's pen."

Steuben punched a few keys on the keyboard then looked up to the large center screen. One alien was in the pen sitting on one of the cots. The other four were nowhere to be seen.

"Confirm that pen is secure then roll the footage from the last hour," Stoner commanded. After confirming that the pen auto locked when the alarm sounded, Steuben accessed the prior footage. The screen flickered alive to show all five aliens in the pen, just as they were when Ro was summoned on the medical call. Exactly as they were.

"Look familiar?" Stoner asked Ro. "This looks like the footage I was shown from prior to the medical emergency," answers Ro. "If I'm right, we'll see two aliens drop about... now."

As if on cue, the two female aliens are seen on camera dropping to the floor. "Explain," is all Stoner says. Jake and Steuben look at each other and then at Ro before Jake says,"We'll need to run some diagnostics sir. At this point you know as much as we do. The only reason the alarm sounded was because for some reason the sound wave blocker went down. We can't be sure whether or not that alien controlled the camera and/or what we were seeing. Either the cameras have been inoperable since the footage was first captured, or the footage has been running on a loop."

Ro steps closer to Stoner. "Maybe neither. What if there was a malfunction that occurred at the same time the alarm sounded and that it affected the older camera footage?" "That's what our tests will hopefully confirm or debunk ma'am," Jake offers.

"Any idea why that one didn't leave the pen with the others?" Stoner gestures to the lone alien in the pen on the screen" "Not a clue sir," Jake responded.

"When the others are recaptured, I want guards situated just outside the pen gate. Contact me when you have answers to how this clusterfuck happened." Stoner took out his phone to text the search party. "Let's go," he said as he led Ro out the door.

Once they were in the corridor, Stoner turned around to Ro and said, "If I find out that you've been holding out on me, I'll see to it that your days of practicing medicine are over. I will finish your career Ro. You know I can do it with just a few calls. You and Basque will be selling Halloween masks at Halloweenmart. Do you understand me? Now, I'm going to ask you this only once and I want you to think before you answer. Why were you first summoned to the Zoo and what do you know about the alien's escape."

As they walked toward the Receiving Bay, Ro explained that she had fully intended to brief Stoner; but, there had not been the opportunity to do so. She went on that she didn't think the captains monitoring the Zoo had the proper clearance so she thought it best to wait until they were alone and knew the extent of the current situation. Stoner seemed to relax a little as she went on to share every detail about the emergency call summoning her to the Zoo. Lucky for her they reached the Receiving Bay before she had to continue.

When they walked in, they were just in time to see the four aliens standing in front of four open portals. Stoner only had time to raise his right hand and yell "STOP!" The four aliens stepped through the portals. Once through, they all four vanished without leaving a trace. The portals closed as soon as they went through. If they hadn't witnessed it, Stoner and Ro may never have known what became of the escapees.

Now that the four are gone there was no need to go into any further detail about how she and Basque helped them at this point. Stoner is not going to let this go Ro thought. I have to give him something, if only to buy some time. Oh God, if he gets to Basque before I can this might be impossible. The son of a bitch could end my career! Think Ro think!

"I think what we just saw confirms that the aliens were able to repair their portable one-way portal packs sir. I believe that they wanted to go back to PCb before the arrival of the Federation sir. I'm sure they are afraid of what will happen to them if they are here when their Federation arrives."

"So you knew they had repaired the portable portal packs and you didn't tell me?" "I just learned about this during my emergency call this morning sir. They didn't tell me where they had hidden the portable packs, just that they brought them here from Base 08 where they had been repaired. These aliens sir? They are the equivalent in age to twenty-five year olds on Earth. They are kids really. Kids soon to be parents and they are trying to do what they think is best for their mates and for their future offspring."

Ro continued. "Once they knew that the fertilization vaccine had worked they became desperate to go back to PCb because the gestation period had reached the final days. That's what caused the emergency. The two females were in early labor. They were afraid to deliver their offspring here because they had probed your mind and learned of your alliance with the PCb Federation. The alliance you made to turn them in for their actions against their ship commander. They just wanted the chance to have their offspring in peace."

Then, Ro reminded Stoner of something she hoped would save her career. "The fifth alien agreed to take the heat from their Federation and give the others a chance to escape. They have a large number of supporters on PCb that will protect them. One such supporter has a position of high authority there and could help you achieve an agreement between the Order and the PCb Federation. So, you see the advantage here right Stoner? You still have an alien to hand over to their Federation. We now have the technology to open the Moon Portal. Everyone wins sir. Everyone."

"Maybe not everyone Ro. There are other considerations." Stoner shook his head and frowned at her. "Did it not occur to you that there may be other aspects to this mission of which you are not aware?" "Seriously Stoner? You know damn well none of us is aware of everything, except maybe you." Ro started to walk away.

Stoner reached out and grabbed her upper arm, turning her back around to face him. "I'm not finished with you Ro! Since when were you authorized to give the vaccine to the females in custody and then neglect to inform me of the progress or success of your trial? I trusted your discretion generally, but it goes without saying that I would expect you not to withhold  information of that importance from me!"

"You are right. I got caught up in the excitement of the success we experienced and I over stepped my position.

Truth is, I just confirmed the pregnancies this morning. I was still processing the situation. I intended to fill you in once I knew that the females were stable. You can understand why right? This is huge Stoner! Bigger than we could have hoped for! The success of the vaccine is really a great victory for all of us. You, me, the whole team."

Ro stopped talking and gave Stoner a hard look. "I understand that you're under a great deal of pressure; but, with all due respect, sometimes you can be a bit of a dick, sir."

"Sometime like now Ro?" "Yes! No! Wait, I, I'm just excited about this Stoner. It's my life's work. Please don't deny me this triumph."

"That's just it Ro, you talk in terms of you and this mission is not only about you. You are one of the best. Why the hell do you think I hand picked you for the team? All that aside, you are just one component of the team I built. I built the team Ro! Remember your place or lose it. Are we clear?" Ro nodded her agreement then asked,"What now?"

"Now we get the damn portal open. I'll text Sam and Steve. You text the others and tell them to report here. You stay and fill them in on the escape of the four aliens. Tell them what we witnessed. That's ALL you fill them in on, understand?" You keep them here and wait for me. Can you do that? Can you just follow a simple order Ro?"

Ro sighed heavily and hung her head. When she heard the door open she looked up and gave him a second finger salute to the back of his head while watching him leave.

## Opening the Moon Portal

Stoner found James and Mathew running tests on the robots when he returned to the Reactor Bay. Sam and Steve walked in right behind him.

Stoner began with saying, "Four of the aliens escaped." "Four escaped sir?" James glanced at Mathew then back to Stoner. "Are you going to tell me that you two know something?" "No, not really, it's just seems odd that if they could escape they would leave one of their kind behind," added James.

"Well it ain't like they had much of a choice being that they used individual portal packs to do it and it seems that there were only four operational. The alien left behind may have volunteered to stay." "Is there a protocol we should follow to address their escape sir?" James stepped forward. "Do you want us to secure the security footage from the Zoo and Receiving Bay? We can have the bots analyze it quickly."

"I witnessed their escape from the Receiving Bay. We have personnel in the Zoo, and we know that the security footage there was tampered with. We also know that the sound barrier was rendered inoperable long enough to allow the escape to go unnoticed. The only thing we don't know is how they were able to do it and where the portable portal packs were stashed before the escape. But, that's not priority intel right now, considering they've already escaped. It's done. Now, we need to focus on the present. We need to get the transmitter and receiver up and running. Set the wave length and open the moon portal. We need to do it quickly and without error. I want a flawless run on this."

Stoner continues. "Have you confirmed that the reactor radiation levels have remained within tolerance range after the last test?" Both Texans nodded a yes as they uttered one out loud. "Good! Sam and Steve will stay here and monitor the situation. Sam will give you the go ahead after she confirms to me that the system is a go run. I'm going back to the Receiving Bay where the rest of the team is preparing for the arrival of the PCb Federation. If anything goes wrong, ANYTHING, you shut the system down and alert me." "Roger that sir," Matthew agreed then gave Stoner a proper officer salute.

Stoner opened the door and gave one final order before he left. "Contact Grin and Smith and instruct them to bring our prisoner to the Receiving Bay."

Sam and Steve took positions at the computer control panel while Matthew and James moved the robots into position near the sound transmitter, then returned to the isolation booth. If anything went array, the booth would provide a protective barrier.

"Ready ma'am," James nodded to Sam. "Oh God James, ma'am? Really?" Sam put in her system access password then began to type the instructions for system start up. "I thought you fellas liked me." She continued entering a series of numbered sequences then looked up, "It's a go now or go home guys." James answered with a grin on his face. "You mean go big or go home?" "Whatever works dude, as long as it works and as long as you never call my wife ma'am again," Steve said with a smile thrown Sam's way.

## The PCb Federation Arrives

Once back in the Receiving Bay, Stoner took charge by giving each member of the A.T.E. present specific instruction as to their role when the PCb Federation delegates arrive.

A short time later Stoner receive a text confirmation from Sam. The transmitter is working and the portal should open at any time now. The team witnessed a large circular portal open in the back of the cargo hold. The entire rear of the cargo hold was transformed into a glowing moon gate. Piercing through the silence, Stoner could be heard shouting, "No one goes near the portal!"

Griff, Ro, Basque, Gretchen, and Finn stood perfectly still and in awe. After all they had experienced on this mission they were somewhat conditioned to strange happenings; but, nothing could have prepared them for this.

The first four to step through the portal were likely members of the Grendolan guard, evidenced by the staffs they each carried, the golden bands worn on both upper limbs, and the small golden triangle between their eyes in the center of the headdress sitting squarely atop their heads.

They were followed by two Grendolan Delegates draped in long gold colored capes covered in symbols that appeared to be woven from blue and green metallic thread. One of these was the missing sixth alien commander that had crashed in the Arizona desert years earlier. For the second time it scanned Stoner's mind for information and for the second time Stoner was unaware.

As if by some irresistible force, Stoner found himself sending a text to Sam. A few minutes later Sam and Steve entered the bay. Just behind them, Mathew and Captain Grin escorted the fifth alien into the bay. When it saw the commander it had betrayed, it immediately assumed a prone position.

The guardsmen took custody of the fifth alien by securing it with a wrist band that appeared to totally prohibit it from movement without one of the guardsmen's lead. It was led to the side and flanked by a guard on each side. The delegates nodded to the guardsmen as they went back through the portal with the fifth alien.

Stoner was visibly shaken after seeing the fifth alien depart. There goes my bargaining chip he thought. What the fuck do I do now? He looked around to his team, to Sam and Steve, and shook his head. It's gone wrong! I've lost and can't fix it!

As Stoner squirmed with thoughts of his failure, a thought loud and clear entered his head. It was as though someone was standing right next to him and speaking. "Now you negotiate an alliance. But before you can do that, before I will allow any negotiation, you must come clean. You must cleanse the air here by speaking the truth."

Stoner looked up to see the Grendolan Ambassador and Federation representative walk through the portal.

The others may have guessed, but Ro and Basque immediately knew that the ambassador was female. It wore a gold colored robe that was gathered below the head on each side and had the same blue and green stitched symbols as the robes worn by the delegates. It looked like a reptilian Egyptian goddess, adorned with a gold band around its head that was centered with a bejeweled golden triangle.

This alien was no doubt the one to which Stoner would present the terms provided by the Order to negotiate the alliance on behalf of the human race. Stoner bowed his head to her and the others followed.

## No More Secrets

The Federation Ambassador walked over to Ro and touched the front of her head to Ro's forehead. Suddenly, everything made sense to Ro. The words of the Havasupai Elder came back to her, but this time with the clarity of understanding their meaning.

While's her mind flooded with new information, the world around her came into focus, like when a weather front clears the air. Ro sensed peace and great gratitude from the ambassador.

During this mind share Ri learned that one of the females she had vaccinated is the offspring of the ambassador and that the ambassador was overjoyed to discover of the pregnancy.

The secret alliance she and Basque had formed with the four escaping aliens was no longer a secret. Ro felt the relief of letting the burden of that secret go.

When the moment ended, the ambassador backed away from Ro, nodded to both her and Basque, then turned to face the others who had been silently watching.

The ambassador alien walked over to Sam and Steve and took each by the hand as she spoke to their minds. "You are about to be shocked. You must try to remain calm while you adjust. Your love for each other will help you adjust quickly. It will help you all."

Sam was visibly confused. She leaned toward Steve and looked at him wanting confirmation that he had heard the same message as she had. When he nodded to her, she realized that he had. What happened next took everyone by surprise.

The ambassador walked Sam and Steve over to the still opened portal then went through with both of them flanking her on either side.

Griff was the first to break the silence. “Stoner, what the hell is going on here? Did you know about this? Was this a part of your plan? Where did the ambassador take Sam and Steve and why?”

“Take it easy Griff. I’m as surprised by this as you are, though I was hoping…” “Hoping for what you son of a bitch! Hoping to sacrifice our team for your own selfish gain?”

Having said that, Griff made a sudden leap toward Stoner that would have at any other time clocked him good. Lucky for Stoner, the move was stopped by the two remaining guardsmen.

With Griff still trying to get to him, Stoner said, “I was hoping that I could exchange the alien we had for, for…” The guardsmen put pressure on Stoner’s neck as Stoner collapsed while finishing, “for my granddaughter!”

Movement at the portal caught everyone’s attention. As if on cue, the Federation Ambassador, Sam, and Steve holding a sleeping Maddie in his arms walked back through the portal and into The Receiving Bay. Maddie lie still with a stuffed dog toy tucked under her chin and crossed arms.

Stoner was stunned. The child looked as though she hadn’t aged a day since her disappearance. Ro went to them and gently touched Steve's arm. "Bring her to the Medical Bay where I can examine her Steve. Sam, do you want to join us now or . . . " Ro glances over at Stoner. The others are still taken back by his announcement.

Sam walks over to Stoner and slaps him hard across his face. "I've wanted to do that for a long time." While Stoner collects himself, Sam goes back to Steve and Maddie. She strokes Maddie's hair then says, "I can't leave her Ro." Ro puts an arm around her and moves toward the exit as she says, "Let's go."

The Alien Ambassador moves toward the portal. Everyone heard her silent words of farewell. "Until the next pleasure. My delegates and guardsmen will stay to complete the negotiations for an Earth exit portal route in exchange for our use of Base 08 as a vaccination center." She lifted both arms in a gesture of peace then turned to step back through the portal.

The guardsman released his hold on Stoner, who immediately ran to the Sam and the others headed toward the exit. As the portal closed Stoner heard one last message. "Remember, no more secrets."

Stoner caught up to Sam and began his confession."I know I had that slap coming Sam. I don't blame you. If you just give me a chance to explain. I don't know where to start Sam. Maybe we can go somewhere more private?" "No," Sam cut him off. "No! Stoner, you can stay away from us. We don't need to see your face anywhere near us!" Steve touches Sam's arm, presses two fingers to his lips, then points to Maddie.

As they made their way to the Medical Bay, Stoner persists in following them. He keeps up with their pace walking right behind Ro, and continues.

He blurts out to her that he is her father and that he did all the things to manipulate her life in order to make sure that he could keep her close. He tells her he wanted to protect her and that her mother agreed that maintaining the secret of their alliance was necessary.

He told her about his discovery that Maddie was taken by the sixth alien commander on board the spaceship that crashed in the desert. He told her about his plan to get her back and about his alliance with the aliens. He told her everything.

"I didn't have much of a choice Sam. We needed to get the Moon Portal open to have any chance of seeing Maddie again. I wanted to tell you but it wouldn't have done any good. It would have caused more worry and anxiety. You can see that can't you? I know I haven't been a good father to you at all times but I have done everything I could to keep you safe and to bring Maddie back. The only sound he heard in reply was the sound of their footsteps in the corridor. "Say something Sam, say anything! Please. . ." Stoner's voice cracked. It was the first time that Sam witnessed him as a vulnerable human and not the sword wielding asshole she grew up to know.

Sam waits until the others are inside the Medical Bay and beyond earshot before she faces Stoner and continues. "Say something Stoner? Really? Say something? You selfish prick! You haven't always been a good father? Father, Stoner? You're hitting me with this now? All at once? You bastard! You were never my father Stoner! Never there for me like a father should be. Never! I'm processing the fact that my daughter is back. That is all my mind can focus on right now. Steve and I will deal with you later but you should leave us alone right now! Is that enough something for you Stoner?"

Sam opens the door to the Medical Bay, slips through, then swiftly closes and locks the door before Stoner could push his way in behind her.

## A Gift

"How can this be?" Sam looked to Ro for an answer. "Look at her Steve! She is exactly the same as the day she disappeared!" Sam moved close beside Steve standing next to the examination table he had laid Maddie on. Steve put his free arm around Sam without letting go of Maddie's hand. "Do you think it's a side effect of traveling through a portal Ro? Sam's right. Maddie looks like she hasn't aged at all. Is she going to be okay?"

"I'm running diagnostics now," said Ro who was busy punching into a computer next to the bed where Maddie lay perfectly still. "The indicators are all good," she smiled at Sam and Steve. "Maddie is fine. The ambassador told me that her physical form was preserved throughout her time on PCb. For her transport back from PCb she was put in a suspended state of consciousness. Time passes differently on PCb; but, Maddie was not at all affected by the passage of time."

Ro went on. "It's extraordinary to witness a human in suspended state of consciousness. A miraculous situation really. From a medical standpoint this is the kind of advanced technology our race still dreams of. We will have access to this technical knowledge and more now. Thanks to the team and the success of our mission. The alien ambassador was grateful that we were able to develop the fertilization vaccine." Ro stopped there, deciding that it was best to not reveal any more information just yet.

Ro hesitated, then continued, "I didn't understand all the details the ambassador shared; but, their race is able to stop the aging process in young offspring. They were hoping that this ability would provide the time they needed to cure the infertility in their females. But, sadly, this ability was a just a byproduct of their evolutionary advancements, the outcome of which, unfortunately, rendered their females infertile."

"Until now," Basque chimed in. So much for keeping our success close to the vest, thought Ro. "That's right," Ro confirmed. "The vaccine we developed and administered to two of their females worked. This morning I discovered that both are carrying offspring. I've estimated that they have already delivered their young, likely just after returning home through the portal." "That's why they were in such a hurry to get back to their home planet," added Basque.

"There's more," Ro went on. "Basque and I agreed to help them escape in order that they could get back to PCb unencumbered by the guards sent to escort them back to be arrested for their crimes. The alien that stayed behind agreed to take the heat; but, we know it's only a matter of time before they others will be caught. We have reason to believe that the four aliens will be all right. What I'm about to tell you must stay secret from Stoner and the others."

Ro drew in a deep breath. "The alien ambassador told me that one of the females was her offspring. This female and another of their species stowed away on the spacecraft that crashed in the desert.  The commander and three of their species were on a reconnaissance mission when their spacecraft crashed. The two female stowaways were mated with two of the male aliens aboard the craft. Now that they have all returned to PCb, the ambassador will do what she needs to do in order to protect them."

Basque explained further. “We provided the time they needed to safely birth their offspring when we guarded this secret. After the births, they will be celebrated by their Federation and, although they will still be required to answer for their crime, the punishment will likely be reduced to the equivalent of what we call on Earth “time served” due to their work contribution while on Base 08.”

“How did Stoner know that the aliens had Maddie?” Steve asked.

Basque stepped forward. “Stoner must have been contacted by the captain of the alien ship that crash landed after the captain had taken Maddie. Ro and I think that Stoner devised a scheme to use the aliens in captivity as leverage. He manipulated them into opening the portal on Base 08, then betrayed them in order to get them into captivity before they could open the Moon Base Portal. We believe that he initially intended to hand all five of them over to the PCb Federation.”

“Sure does sound like something Stoner would do. He is the master of manipulation, the son of a bitch,” Sam commented.

Ro took over. “But, while Stoner was busy executing his manipulation scheme. . .” Ro pauses. “The scheme that included his getting credit with the Order for opening the Moon Base Portal and for negotiating an agreement with the PCb Federation to use the Portal as an Earth escape route for likes of those in The Order, Basque and I thwarted his plan by entering into our own alien alliance.

“He still had the remaining alien to use as his bargaining chip,” Steve said as he stood up and crossed his arms. “If he knew that the vaccine was a success, he wouldn't have needed a bargaining chip." "Exactly!," Ro stated. "Stoner didn't know if the vaccine would work and I didn't tell him that it had until the escape of the four aliens was already in progress."

"The alien commander must have probed Stoner's mind and learned of his fraud," Steve said. "That's why they took Maddie!," Sam cried. "The son of a bitch wasn't going to tell us where she was unless he was sure they had her and would deliver her back in exchange for their own." "We don't know that Sam," Basque interjects. "All we really know for sure is that Maddie was taken by the alien and returned. If they were negotiating a hostage exchange they wouldn't have returned Maddie without some confirmation as to the whereabouts of the other four aliens." "But the gratitude expressed by the ambassador belies that reasoning Basque," Ro concludes. "I do agree that Stoner gambled. He had no way of knowing for sure that they would bring her back. He just wanted his mission to be a success, no matter what the consequences," Steve said while shaking his head. "Classic Stoner M.O.," added Sam.

The all turned their attention back to Maddie. With his gaze fixed on her, Steve asked, "How do we wake her Ro? She looks like Sleeping Beauty." "No Steve!" Sam cries. "Sleeping Beauty was dead and Maddie is just in a suspended sleep, right Ro?"

Sam got up and started pacing around the room while Ro spoke. "Right Sam. Try to stay calm. Maddie will wake up, but here's the tricky part." Ro sat down in a chair and motioned for Sam and Steve to sit. She then moved close to the couple and reached out to take their hands in hers before continuing.

"The Federation is giving you a great gift that requires the two of you to make a decision." Sam interrupts. "The fact that Maddie is back unharmed is a gift, for sure. However, considering the fact that she was kidnapped by a Grendolan Commander and used as leverage on Stoner, I question the integrity of the Grendolans, generally. While I do want to trust that their ambassador is on the up and up, I am still leery of those in charge of the PCb Federation." "It seems that their "in command" are no different than ours," Steve mutters. "Ever the hidden agenda," Sam adds. "Perhaps now, with the Federation and the Oder reaching an agreement, we can move forward aligned in our objectives," offers Ro.

Ro goes on. "When I said gift I was referring to a choice that is being given to you. A choice regarding how Maddie will awaken." "She won't just wake up?" asked Sam. "Yes she will wake up but to what reality," answered Ro.

"Let me explain further," Ro says after getting puzzled looks from each Steve and Sam. "Specifically, your decision is regarding Maddie's memory. In other words, do you want her to have no recollection of her kidnapping and the time she was held on PCb? If you choose this, Maddie will awaken believing it is the same day at the same time when she disappeared. She will still be running through the corn field on your farm. Running on her way to the lower acreage to find her father exercising the horses."

Ro pauses to allow what she said to register then continues. "Of course this option would require that you both return to the farm and restore It to appear just as it was when Maddie disappeared. The two of you would also return to that moment in time, although you would still have full recollection of the past, from the moment Maddie disappeared forward."

"The other option?" asked Steve. "The other option is that Maddie remembers her kidnapping and the time she spent on PCb, including what occurs there during her time in the suspended state. She will have memory of being in a sub-conscience state; but, that memory will likely be similar to that one has while dreaming. Real, but not real. Regardless of the decision, Maddie may need therapy if not now, at some future point in time. We cannot be certain that there will not be some latent residual affects on her. On the brighter side, children are known to have adaptation capabilities that outshine most adults."

Basque takes over the lead on the conversation. "With the bonus we each earned on this project you can completely start over if you like. You can return to the farm or go somewhere else. You can decide how you will move forward. You can live together as a family or live apart as separate parents."

Ro finishes. "I understand this is a lot to process. I wish I could tell you that you can take your time; but, according to what the ambassador told me, you only have 48 hours to decide before Maddie will awaken."

## Nine Months Later

Sam picked up a young tomato plant and gently placed it in one of the troweled holes set in a row before her. She filled in the hole, pressing down the soil with her gloved hands, then, she placed a thin wooden stake near enough to the hole in order to tie and steady the plant as it grew.

Steve appeared at the kitchen door with a wide-brimmed hat in his hand. “You forgot this babe. I don’t want my wife getting sunburned,” he said as he crossed over to her and placed it on her head. “Thanks. What would I do without you love,” Sam smiles up at Steve then raises to stand before him.

“You going to start to break in the new stallions this morning?” “I think I’ll save that for our company. What time did you tell them to come?” “I said anytime after 3:00 pm, but you know Stoner will be here early. Any chance he gets to see Maddie...” Steve cuts her off. “A chance to show some gratitude for your forgiveness...” This time Sam’s cuts Steve off. “Oh no! He is not totally off the hook yet! He has to earn your forgiveness too.”

As Sam speaks, Steve adds a “uh huh” after each sentence like he’s heard her justify herself before. He knows the drill. Sam will state the truth until she convinces herself to accept it.

“The confession was a good start, and we both agree that he was in a very bad position. It’s not as though he caused the aliens to crash land. Even if he had come clean about our relationship sooner, how would that have prevented Maddie from being kidnapped? How would it have helped us to know she had been abducted and taken to another planet?"

Sam goes on. "Stoner is trying. He bought Maddie the purebred Aussie Shepherd and brokered the deal on the new stallions for the farm. I know that he still has to prove himself. He has to show us through his actions that he will not try to manipulate our lives in even the smallest way if he wants to be a part of this family."

"That's one reason I love you more every day, my companionate wife," Steve says as he tenderly cups her shoulders and leans in to kiss her full on the mouth. "What were we just talking about?" Sam looks deep into Steve's eyes and sighs. "You still send me Mr. Mansion. I'll have more of those kisses anytime." Sam gives Steve a warm hug then says, "Oh yes, what time our friends are coming," Sam says with a giggle.

"We know that Gretchen and Finn will be the last to arrive. Their watches are always set on delayed o'clock. If Ro and Basque ride with them like they usually do, they'll all meander here by 4:30 or so in the afternoon. Griff will be here before 2:00, probably at noon, carrying two dozen donuts in one hand and a large coffee in the other. He will ask you to help him carry what I'll wager to guess will be the largest prize pig in the county."

"Yeah," Steve chuckles. "Between him and our favorite Texans, it'll be interesting to see who wins the spot at the large grill."

"That one is easy! Griff for sure. Especially when you divert Mathew and James to the lower acreage. They will gladly give up the grilling post when they learn that there are two new horses to break in."

"That reminds me, we really should help Maddie break in her new puppy, I think we need to set some house rules. I caught the pup chewing another of her shoes this morning. If she crated the pup at night, it would limit his morning free-roving tendencies."

"Agreed. Lets talk to her before bedtime." Steve continues. "Has she given you any hint of what she wants to name it?" "Almost every time I see her," Sam says with a laugh. "Let's see, uh, (Sam places her forefinger under her chin) just this morning she called him Rossi the amazing Aussi."

"Sounds more like the title of a cartoon episode," Steve comments. "Exactly! She's was so funny about it too. Just started addressing the pup that way out of the blue. Then expected it to understand that she just gave it a name and that it must listen to her and be at attention if she says it again." "Well,"starts Steve, "Australian Shepherds are a very intelligent dog breed. It will figure her out." "Or just answer to her voice no matter what she says," Sam concludes.

Steve looks around the yard then says, "I should go check in on the two of them. Any idea where Maddie went with him?" "She had the pup in a doll stroller and was heading toward the greenhouse about fifteen minutes ago."

"The greenhouse? Again? She's been going there every day. If she's in there, I'll bring her out. It's pretty humid in there. The pup won't like it for long." "Okay love. I'm going to finish planting these then get cleaned up and start lunch."

Steve walks over to the greenhouse and opens door. The space is filled with lush tropical plants and flowers. A water stream cascades at one end into an irrigation system that snakes around the paving stones that form a walking path. There are a few exotic birds free to fly about in an aviary near the top of the atrium portion of the building. Finches, small parrots, quails, and sparrows can be heard chattering as he enters.

He calls out for his daughter. “Maddie, your puppy is going to be hot if he stays in here for long. Now come on out from wherever you’re hiding and let’s go outside. It’s a beautiful day and you know that we have company coming. Maddie?”

A soft swooshing sound can be heard in the back of the greenhouse behind the banana trees. As Steve gets closer he can see Maddie with the puppy in her lap sitting on a paving stone in front of the parked doll stroller.

Then he sees them. Peeking out from behind the planters placed in front of the banana trees are three small alien Grendolans, each wearing a thin sash that was slung around the top portion of their body. Affixed to the lowest part of the sash was a small pouch, golden in color, matching the band they each wore around the wrist of their left webbed hand-like appendage.

The puppy yips at the site of Steve then jumps playfully at the small aliens. “Daddy, not yet! We’re playing!” “One more minute Maddie, then that’s all for today. You can play together again soon.” ”Aw! But daddy these are my friends!” “Maddie you heard me, just a minute longer. Hello to you three too!” He waves to the young aliens then looks back to Maddie and asks,”Is their nanny here?” Maddie laughs.

“Daddy you know they don't have nannies! They have walkie talkies that pull them back home when they have to leave.” Maddie gets up and darts behind the line of potted plants after the aliens and her pup.

A minute later Steve reaches in behind the planters and pulls Maddie out with one hand and the pup out with the other. “Okay, Maddie, say goodbye for now.” He waves again to the aliens and puts the pup back in the doll stroller.

As he’s walking Maddie toward the greenhouse exit he turns in time to see the golden pouches begin to glow. The gold bands worn by the small aliens get brighter and brighter as a thin thread of light snakes out of each pouch to form a circle in front of them. The circles of light steadily widen until each is large enough for the young aliens to move through.

Maddie stops and turns just in time to wave a goodbye. “See ya soon okay?” An instant later, the aliens slip through and the portals close. That never gets old, Steve thought to himself.

## References

National Association for Gifted Children, Assessments & Tests nagc.org (accessed 12/30/25).

MIT First year catalogue; Department of Physics catalog; MIT Kavli Institute for Astrophysics and Space Research catalog.mit.edu; physics.mit.edu (accessed 8/8/25).

Department of Psychology, School of Humanities and Sciences psychology.stanford.edu (accessed 8/13/25).

“throwing a lasso” answers.com (accessed 7/22/25).

*Talk the Talk Essential Ranch Slang and Cowboy Lingo,Western Slang, Lingo, and Phrases* - A Writer's Guide to the Old West - Legends of America; Fun with Words - Cowboy Slang, Lingo, and Jargon - The Chief Storyteller, starduneranch.com (accessed 12/30/25).

Andrew J Kwok, Alex Mentzer, Julian C Knight *Host Genetics and Infectious Disease: new tools insights and translational* opportunities; Nature Reviews Genetics Vil 22 (March 2021).

*Medical Research at Oxford*; school of Medicine and Biomedical Sciences; Human Sciences ox.ak.uk (accessed 8/21/25).

Scientific Reports, Psychology top 100 2023 nature.com (accessed 8/13/25).

“Trends in Psychology” link.springer.com (accessed 8/13/25).

The American Journal of Psychology jstor.org (accessed 8/13/25).

Conference next.com; International Conference on Psychological, Educational, Health and Social Sciences worldacademics.net (accessed 8/22/25).

Oxford Language Dictionary: dexterous;
Wikipedia: genome, lassi, mechanism inside a transmitter of sound, Proxima Centauri b, transmitter, Pyramid of Menkaure, particle of light.observer effect, Havasupai en.m.wikipedia.org (accessed between 8/1/25-12/30/25).

Time and Date: March 2040 Calendar United States, https://www.timeanddate.com (accessed 9/30/25).

Pai word set languages.org (accessed 9/30/25).

Havasupai word list archive.library.nau.edu (accessed 10/22/25).

Colorado plateau digital collections; Havasupai word list https://archive.library.nau.edu (accessed 3/4/25).

"Native Languages of the Americas" https://www.native-languages.org> pai.htm; Yavapai-Hualapai-Havasupai Indian Language (Pai, Walapai) (accessed 9/30/25).

"Supai the most remote village in the United States" northernarizonaluving.com (accessed 8/30/25).

"Supai: An Isolated Indian Village Inside the Grand Canyon" https://www.amusingplanet.com/2015/03.

## About the Author

Carol Melber is an Author and Independent Publisher living in Florida. This is her ninth book and second science fiction title. Other published books by Carol:

The Rolling Moon

Jumping Jellybeans

On Love Poems from the Heart

Charlie's Avocado

On Life Path of a Woman's Soul

Paxter the Foster

Texting with a Stranger the true story of a Celebrity Imposter Romance Scam

The Kibble Caper

www.ingramcontent.com/pod-product-compliance
Lightning Source LLC
LaVergne TN
LVHW010918110826
845149LV00013B/2414

* 9 7 8 0 9 9 8 3 4 8 6 3 6 *